Sun...

Can you take the heat?

Love is in the air and the forecasts have promised a spell of sun, sea and sizzling romance. So let us whisk you away to this season's most glamorous destinations full of rolling hills, blissful beaches and piping hot passion! Take your seat and follow as these sun-kissed couples find their forever on faraway shores. After all, it's been said you should catch flights, not feelings—but who says you can't do both?

Start your journey to true love in...

The Venice Reunion Arrangement
by Michelle Douglas

Dating Game with Her Enemy
by Justine Lewis

The Billionaire She Loves to Hate
by Scarlett Clarke

Cinderella's Greek Island Temptation
by Cara Colter

A Reunion in Tuscany
by Sophie Pembroke

Their Mauritius Wedding Ruse
by Nina Milne

Available now!

And look out for the next stop of your travels with...

Fake Date on the Orient Express
by Jessica Gilmore

Coming soon!

Dear Reader,

Over the years, I've written a lot of seasonal stories—ones filled with Christmas sparkle, or crisp fall vibes, or the freshness of spring. But I think there's something about the magic of summer that is just perfect for romance.

For Luca and Daphne in this story, it's a return to the place they fell for each other fifteen years ago, when they were twenty-one. It's a chance to relive those heady summer days of their holiday fling...or could it be something more this time?

Summer is a time for dreamers and lovers. I hope you enjoy this story about dreaming big dreams and trusting in love to make them happen.

Love and sunshine,

Sophie x

A REUNION IN TUSCANY

SOPHIE PEMBROKE

ROMANCE

If you purchased this book without a cover you should be aware that this book is stolen property. It was reported as "unsold and destroyed" to the publisher, and neither the author nor the publisher has received any payment for this "stripped book."

ISBN-13: 978-1-335-21646-5

Recycling programs for this product may not exist in your area.

A Reunion in Tuscany

Copyright © 2025 by Sophie Pembroke

All rights reserved. No part of this book may be used or reproduced in any manner whatsoever without written permission.

Without limiting the author's and publisher's exclusive rights, any unauthorized use of this publication to train generative artificial intelligence (AI) technologies is expressly prohibited.

This is a work of fiction. Names, characters, places and incidents are either the product of the author's imagination or are used fictitiously. Any resemblance to actual persons, living or dead, businesses, companies, events or locales is entirely coincidental.

For questions and comments about the quality of this book, please contact us at CustomerService@Harlequin.com.

TM and ® are trademarks of Harlequin Enterprises ULC.

Harlequin Enterprises ULC
22 Adelaide St. West, 41st Floor
Toronto, Ontario M5H 4E3, Canada
www.Harlequin.com

Printed in U.S.A.

Sophie Pembroke has been dreaming, reading and writing romance ever since she read her first Harlequin novel as part of her English literature degree at Lancaster University, so getting to write romantic fiction for a living really is a dream come true! Born in Abu Dhabi, Sophie grew up in Wales and now lives in a little Hertfordshire market town with her scientist husband, her incredibly imaginative and creative daughter, and her adventurous, adorable little boy. In Sophie's world, happy *is* forever after, everything stops for tea and there's always time for one more page...

Books by Sophie Pembroke

Harlequin Romance

Blame It on the Mistletoe

Christmas Bride's Stand-In Groom

Dream Destinations

Their Icelandic Marriage Reunion
Baby Surprise in Costa Rica

Twin Sister Swap

Cinderella in the Spotlight
Socialite's Nine-Month Secret

Winter Escapes

Copenhagen Escape with the Billionaire

The Princess and the Rebel Billionaire
Best Man with Benefits

Visit the Author Profile page
at Harlequin.com for more titles.

For my lovely readers,
may all your dreams come true this summer!

Praise for
Sophie Pembroke

"An emotionally satisfying contemporary romance full of
hope and heart, *Second Chance for the Single Mom* is
the latest spellbinding tale from Sophie Pembroke's very
gifted pen. A poignant and feel-good tale that touches
the heart and lifts the spirits."
—*Goodreads*

CHAPTER ONE

DAPHNE BROWN COULD already feel the disappointing grey of the London summer day she'd started out in fading away as the Tuscan sunshine beat down. Yes, she was only standing outside the airport in Florence, waiting for a minibus or something to take her to her destination, but even an Italian airport felt more exotic than London Gatwick had that morning.

She'd really done it. She'd left the UK— only for five days, but still. It was something she hadn't managed in too long—despite her youthful dreams of one day making a name for herself as a travel writer.

A travel writer who didn't travel was just a writer. And Daphne hadn't even done any *writing* worth the name in the last ten years or so. But in her bag right now was a brand-new hardback notebook and pen, and already she could feel the pull to write coming over her.

She breathed in the warm, sun-infused air and mentally noted all the ways her senses were reacting to her surroundings so she could write them down as soon as they got to wherever it was they were staying. It was the little details—the odd things she spotted that no one else had, or the way a certain scent or sound made her *feel*—that would make her writing stand out. At least, that was what her old professor at university had told her. He'd wanted her to go back and study for a master's in creative writing after she'd graduated but, well... That hadn't happened.

Beside her, her best friend Erin nudged her knowingly. 'I told you this was a good idea.'

'You did. Repeatedly.' Erin had been bugging her about doing a girls' trip for literally years, and in the aftermath of her latest breakup, Daphne had finally run out of arguments.

Okay, that wasn't true. She still had plenty of reasons why she should still be at home, keeping the family business on track—not to mention the actual family.

But she'd really, really wanted to go.

'Be selfish for once,' Erin had begged, her finger hovering over the 'book now' button on the airline website. 'Come with me. You need a break. You *deserve* a break.'

And Daphne had let herself believe that she did. At least, for long enough for Erin to press that button, plug in Daphne's credit card details for the flight only, and present the rest of her trip plans as a *fait accompli*.

'I already know exactly what we'll be doing while we're there,' she'd told her, beaming. 'I have the whole thing planned—and paid for. Call it my birthday present to you. You're going to *love* it.'

And now they were there. In Italy. The last place she'd ever felt free.

Already, reminiscences were pressing against her brain, begging to be relived. Memories of dancing in the moonlight of an olive grove, strong arms wrapped around her. Of sitting watching the sunset with a gelato in hand, feeling like the whole world was just out there waiting for her. For Daphne Brown.

Except instead, she'd gone home to her family home in London, and stayed there. For fifteen long years.

She caught herself in the thought and bent down to fiddle with the zips of her suitcase instead, checking they were closed. She was being ungrateful. She had a good life—a great life. She'd been twenty-one the last time she was in Italy—a completely different person to the woman she was now at thirty-six. She had *responsibilities* now…

'I should call home.' Her phone was in her hand before she even finished articulating the thought.

Erin grabbed it from her before she could

dial. 'No. You have to convince me first. *Why* do you need to call home?'

'To check on things!' Obviously. Erin— happily married to a man who loved her and their children boundlessly, and with both sets of grandparents around to help out with child-care if needed while she was away—didn't understand. Daphne might not have the husband or the children, but she had other obligations. Ones that mattered to *her*.

'What things?' Erin pressed. 'Who— exactly—are you going to call?'

Daphne paused. 'Well... I guess I'd start with Scott? He's still so new, and this is the first time he's had to take care of the shop without me.' The family printing business had been thriving over the past few years, and she wasn't about to let all that hard work go to waste now, just because she wanted a holiday.

'He's a twenty-six-year-old man who has been working for you for over a year and quite frankly is going to walk away and straight into a new job somewhere else if you don't let him take on some actual responsibility around there,' Erin said bluntly. 'What? We talk while I'm waiting for you to finish up before we go for our Wednesday Night Dinners. Scott is *fine,* and so are the team at the shop. They know what they're doing. So, who else would you call?'

SOPHIE PEMBROKE · 11

'Uh… I should check in with Dad?' She hated that it sounded like a question. *Of course* she should check in with her seventy-six-year-old father. That was just what a responsible eldest daughter should do.

Erin made a buzzer noise. 'No, sorry, that is an incorrect answer. Because you know full well he's staying with your aunt this week and is absolutely fine. Try again.'

'Caitlin might need—'

'Caitlin is a thirty-year-old woman with a network of her own to lean on. The fact that she likes to complain about her life to you does not make her your responsibility.'

'She's my little sister. She'll always be my responsibility.' It was an old argument between the two of them. Caitlin's life always seemed to be filled with small dramas that she needed to share—and let Daphne solve.

'There we will agree to disagree,' Erin said. 'And I know you're going to say Tommy next, but he's also fine. He's thirty-three, Daph, and he'll be at work anyway. Your brother doesn't need you either.'

But if none of them need me…what am I good for?

The thought chilled her, even in the sunshine.

Henry hadn't needed her any more either—that was one of the reasons he'd dumped her.

12 A REUNION IN TUSCANY

'Daph, you've been amazing, a rock,' he'd said as he held her hand, looked into her eyes and ended the relationship she'd really thought was going to lead to a ring this time. 'You were just the woman I needed to get me back on my feet. I can never thank you enough—the past year with you…it's been great. But I feel like now it's time for me to figure out what's next for me on my own. You understand, don't you?'

She understood that now she'd helped him get his confidence back after his divorce and supported him through job-hunting after his redundancy he was ready to go out there and sleep with other women again. As confirmed by watching him out for dinner with a woman half his age in the restaurant she and Erin had coincidentally chosen for one of their Wednesday Night Dinners.

Maybe nobody needed her.

No, that wasn't true. Dad would be home from Aunt Sharon's soon, calling Daphne at the shop to ask about how to fix the telly, or what she was bringing him for dinner. Caitlin would have another crisis of her own making and need her to fix it. And as much as Scott might want more responsibility at the shop, it was a *family* business, always had been, and she was the only family member left working there. Her dad would be heartbroken if that changed, and Caitlin and Tommy had never had any interest in taking it on.

She shook her head to bring herself back to the here and now. She *was* needed. Whether she liked it or not.

Erin slipped a hand through the crook of her arm and pulled her close. 'Right now, the only person who needs you is *me*. *I* need you to relax and enjoy yourself this week. Okay?'

'That would be easier if I knew exactly where we were going,' Daphne grumbled. Florence was all she knew. Erin had told her that if she booked the flight she'd take care of everything else.

'Does it really matter? We're in Tuscany, Daph!' Erin squeezed her arm again and grinned. 'I remember when you came home from that summer you spent here after university—you were like a different person for a while! Tanned and relaxed and confident… Well, except for, you know, everything with your mum. But you always said that summer in Tuscany was the last time you really felt…alive. Free.'

'I didn't say that. Did I?' She'd felt it, sure. But it felt disloyal to her real life to *say* it.

'After you got a few drinks in you, absolutely you did,' Erin replied. 'And I wanted you to feel that way again. Is that so bad?'

'No. Of course it isn't.' Erin had been her

14   A REUNION IN TUSCANY

best friend since primary school. Daphne knew she only ever had her best interests at heart— and she was pretty sure that her husband, Olly, had only encouraged her to take Daphne on this trip. They'd both made enough comments lately, especially in the wake of her last boyfriend fiasco, about her getting out there and living her life for herself for a change. They wanted her to take some time and figure out what she really wanted from life for *herself,* rather than what other people needed from her. Which she appreciated in principle, but...well. It was easier said than done, especially when other people needed so much.

A cheer suddenly went up from the little group who had gathered outside the airport waiting for their transfer. There was a sign in there somewhere that they were waiting by, but Daphne hadn't been able to see it through the small crowd of people. Erin had dipped through to make sure they were in the right place, but insisted that Daphne stay back so as not to spoil the surprise.

Which meant that she really wasn't expecting the limousine that pulled up beside them. Or the logo on the doors.

A house, with a crescent moon shining above it and olive tree branches winding around it as

SOPHIE PEMBROKE

a border. And the words 'Villa della Luna' in a scrawling font below.

'This is it!' Erin squealed. 'I can tell you now! We're going to spend five days at this fantastic cookery school in a real Tuscan villa, learning all about food and doing wine-tastings and—best of all—eating everything we cook. Won't it be incredible!'

'I… I can't believe it,' Daphne said, perfectly honestly, as the driver hopped out, making charming apologies for the delay, and the guests' bags were loaded into the van that had followed behind him.

'And the best bit is the name—that's when I knew we had to go,' Erin went on. 'It's called Villa della Luna—the house of the moon! Isn't that just the most romantic thing you've ever heard? Have you ever even *dreamed* about staying somewhere so romantic?'

Daphne didn't answer. Because she didn't have to dream it.

She'd been there before.

Fifteen years—and a whole lifetime—ago.

Luca Moretti moved easily through the cool passageways of Villa della Luna, before swinging around a sturdy wooden doorframe into the kitchen—Ben's kitchen, he reminded himself. It was easy to believe that all kitchens be-

16 A REUNION IN TUSCANY

longed to him these days, and technically, on the legal documents, this one did. But Ben ran it. Luca was merely a guest here, in the villa he'd bought from Ben's family seven years earlier.

'Are you unpacked?' Ben looked up from where he was examining some meat—pork, Luca thought—with one of his chefs.

'I am. Glad to see my bedroom hadn't been let for the week.' That had happened last time he'd swung by for an unexpected visit. The fifty-something insurance man staying in it hadn't been happy to see him when he arrived in the middle of the night. Luca had ended up staying in one of the staff cabins out by the olive grove for the night—and then decamped to the apartment he kept in Florence the following morning. He probably should have stayed there from the start, but he'd missed his friends. Also, he knew that his Florence kitchen was empty, and there was always fantastic food at all times of the day or night at Villa della Luna.

'It's a small group this week. One late addition—the friend of one of the registered participants—but still only eight in total. We didn't need your room.' Ben looked up and caught his eye, his lips spreading into a suspicious wide smile. 'But since you're here, we can definitely use your expertise! I'm sure our guests would *love* to have a world-famous chef like yourself teaching them to make saltimbocca. Think of the online reviews we'd get for that…'

'I didn't come here to work.' Luca followed Ben out of the doors that led to the terrace, from where they could watch the long, winding road that led to the villa for the arrival of their guests. At the bottom, Luca could see a long black car followed by a smaller one, steadily making their way up the hill.

'Then why *did* you come?' Ben dropped into the swing seat that had been there longer than Luca could remember, and gestured for Luca to join him.

He did. But he sighed so his oldest friend would know he didn't appreciate the interrogation. 'I came to…regroup. And, you know, to check on my investment.' Damn it, should have led with that one.

Buying Ben's family villa when his father went bankrupt had mostly been out of nostalgic fondness for the place, and the fact that he knew Ben loved it so much. Turning it into a cooking school that Ben could run…well, that had been a stroke of unexpected genius that worked out much better than either of them had expected.

Inevitably, Ben ignored any mention of business motives for his visit. 'Regroup? You mean to hide.' He gave Luca a sideways look. 'We do get all the American gossip websites here, you realise.'

Ah. Which was his friend's way of telling him that everyone at the villa already knew about the well publicised row with Serena outside New York's hottest restaurant—his, as it happened—and that his on-again, off-again relationship was probably off again.

No, *definitely* off, and for good this time.

'Want to tell me what happened?' Ben asked. 'I mean, you two are in the papers all the time with people speculating about whether you're getting married or breaking up, but it doesn't usually result in a midnight flight to Italy for you.'

Luca sighed. The convoy bringing the latest students for the cookery school was getting closer, and this really wasn't a conversation he wanted to have around strangers. Better to get it over with now.

'It turned out that this particular altercation had been orchestrated by Serena herself,' Luca explained. 'She'd even invited the photographers ready to capture it. Apparently, she hadn't been in the news enough lately.'

'Wow.' Ben winced. 'That's…cold.'

'That's what celebrity dating looks like.' Luca hadn't set out to be a celebrity. He'd set out to be a success. To show his father that he didn't need his ancestral wealth and company, that he could succeed on his own, being himself, following his own dreams instead of being miserable inside the family property business, building soulless shopping centres, chain restaurants and office blocks all over America.

And he'd done that, too—so successfully that his father had even re-inherited him, if that was such a thing. Written him back into the will he'd been so firmly written out of anyway, the day Luca's culinary empire helped him hit billionaire status.

It wasn't the Michelin stars his—all individually themed—restaurants had earned, or the cookery school he'd set up, or the revenue generating viral social media platforms and websites that had convinced his father of his success. It certainly wasn't the charitable work his popularity and income had allowed him to perform. No, Howard Monroe III only cared about the money. It was those zeroes after his net worth that had made him open his arms and welcome him back into the fold after so many years.

Not that Luca really wanted to be there.

Was it any wonder that his concept of love might be a little warped these days? People were out for what you were worth to them. Always had been, always would be.

'I'm pretty sure that's not what dating—of any sort—is supposed to look like,' Ben said.

'What would you know about it?' Luca asked. 'You and Theo didn't date. You just flirted awkwardly until you fell into bed together, and then you just kept having great sex—loudly, all over the villa, I might add—until one of you agreed to marry the other.' He'd never got their proposal story straight. Given how dramatically Theo blushed when anyone asked about it, Luca was pretty sure he never wanted to know.

Ben, however, beamed smugly. 'What can I say? Me and my man have got love *sorted*.'

The annoying thing was, they really had. 'At least while I'm here we can finalise the last bits for the wedding next month.' Talking about their upcoming nuptials was a surefire way to get Ben off the topic of Luca's love life and onto his own.

'Yes! Because I know Theo wanted to discuss the—' Ben broke off with a frown. 'No. We'll talk about that later. We're talking about *you* now.'

Luca groaned. So much for that plan. 'Do we have to?'

'We do.' Ben twisted on the seat, holding

the swing steady with one foot on the ground, the other folded up under him, and focused his whole attention on Luca. 'Listen. New York is toxic for you right now. I know it was what you needed when you first went there—to grow the brand or whatever it was. And I know you love the new restaurant out there and I'm thrilled it's doing so well but…you're not yourself when you're over there. Theo and I both saw it, when we visited earlier in the year.'

'Is this an intervention?' Luca joked. 'Shouldn't Theo be here if you're going to save me from myself?' Ben was his oldest friend, while he'd only met Theo four years earlier, shortly after they started the school. But Ben's fiancé had already become as close a friend as any others Luca had in the world. And he was always the one who could find the words to say exactly what he needed to hear.

'He would be, but the limo driver begged off sick, so he had to go fetch everyone from the airport.' They both looked out at the road. The limo was larger now, closer. Almost there. Any moment now it would pull up in front of the villa and they'd have to go round and greet the guests and Luca would be saved from this conversation.

'Look, New York isn't for ever,' Luca said, trying to appease his friend. 'The restaurant is thriving. I'll be able to hand it off to someone else soon.'

'And then what?' Ben asked. 'Because I'm not sure that the city that never sleeps is the only problem here. When was the last time you stayed in one place long enough to put down any actual roots? Make friends? Fall in love— not whatever sham dating you and Serena have been up to?'

'Not everyone has a family villa they can retreat to and fall in love with and get married at.' Luca kept his gaze trained on the approaching vehicles.

Nearly there...

'But you do!' Ben jumped to his feet, waving his hands as he stood over Luca, demanding his attention. 'You literally do! You own this place, remember?'

'That's just on paper. An investment. You know this place is yours really. And Theo's soon, I guess.'

Ben rolled his eyes. 'Yes, because you're so famous and successful that you can afford to buy your best friend's family villa and *give* it to him to run a cookery school.'

Luca squinted up through the sunlight. 'You say that like it's a bad thing.'

He frowned. 'Well. Maybe I'm getting off track. The point is...success isn't everything.

You don't have to keep going from one big success to the next, trying to top whatever you did last time. You don't have to pretend to date whoever is hottest or the biggest catch in whatever city you're in. You don't have to keep trying so hard, Luca. Sometimes it's okay to just... stop and enjoy where you are. I mean, when was the last time you did that? Really?'

The vehicles had disappeared from the road now, meaning they'd taken the last corner and would be pulling up at the front of the villa any moment. Ben was breathing hard after his tirade, waiting for Luca's response.

Luca pushed down on the arm of the swing and stood up slowly. He didn't answer Ben's question, even though he knew the answer.

Fifteen years ago, right here at Villa della Luna.

That was the last time he'd felt...himself. He'd had more opportunities thrown his way since than he'd ever had before—more money, more success, more women and accolades. He'd gone out into the world and made it sit up and pay attention to him.

That first summer at the villa, though, between walking out on his father after telling him he'd never join the family business, and starting his own culinary career... That summer had been magical. A moment out of time. Full of wine and sunshine and gelato and moonlight and a woman who turned his world upside down...

That summer had been everything to Luca. And then it was over.

He suspected Ben knew all that, too. He'd been there for it, after all—and for the fallout. Maybe that was why he didn't push any further now.

From somewhere out front, a car door slammed and Theo's voice wafted on the breeze, welcoming their guests to the villa.

'We should go say hello,' Luca suggested. 'Surprise them. See if my mere presence can get you some of those reviews you wanted.'

Ben nodded, and together they made their way down from the terrace and around to the front of the building, where the branded limo and van were now parked.

Luca cast an eye over the latest students— the usual mix of middle-aged men and women, a younger honeymooning couple and a woman who looked older even than his *nonna*. Ben had already gone over to greet them with Theo and introduce himself, but Luca hung back until the last couple of guests had exited the car. There was a thirty-something woman with red hair climbing out of the limo now and behind her...

His heart stopped for what felt like for ever as he watched the next guest shake out her long, curly dark hair, one hand shading her eyes as she looked up at the villa. She looked just like—

But it wouldn't be, of course. It never was.

Over the last fifteen years he'd thought he'd seen her in cities all over the world. Had chased dark-haired women down streets only to realise that their faces were wrong when they turned to look at him in surprise. Their eyes were brown instead of green, or their skin too freckled, their mouths too small, their nose the wrong shape. They were never *her*.

But then the woman turned and saw him, her eyes widening, and he knew.

She didn't just look like her. It *was* her.

'Daphne Brown,' he whispered softly, his heart hammering against his ribcage.

The one woman who had made his whole world stop, fifteen years ago, had returned to Villa della Luna at last. Why? How? Did she even know he owned it? She couldn't have known he'd be here—*he* hadn't known he'd be here until last night.

What had her life been since she'd left? And what on earth could bring her back here now?

Most importantly, though. Would she leave his heart intact this time around?

The winding road up to Villa della Luna was just as Daphne remembered—although last

26 A REUNION IN TUSCANY

time she'd mostly taken it on foot, or bike, or once on the back of a motorcycle, her arms wrapped tight around the rider's waist.

A limo was definitely a new experience.

She tuned out the chatter amongst the group in the car about what would be waiting for them at the top of the hill, instead choosing to imagine how the villa would have changed since her last visit. Ben's family must have sold it somewhere in the last fifteen years, and converted it into the cookery school. That would make sense. She probably wouldn't recognise any of it.

Except she *did*. Even as the car took the last corner and the villa came into full sight her breath caught in her chest just looking at it. Probably the shutters had been given a fresh coat of paint or two, but really, it looked exactly the same. All sun-warmed stone walls and red tiled roof, with olive-green shutters that echoed the hardy plants growing around it, and the leaves of the olive trees in the grove behind. Even the views were the same, looking out over the same hills and fields, the same mix of olive green and terracotta red and sandy yellow brown, undulating through the landscape. The village at the bottom of the hill, with its multi-level roofs and twisting passageways, looked the same too, and memories of days exploring it, of a summer spent selling gelato in the café there, floored her as the others got out of the car.

She *knew* this place. She'd written about this place, poured it out onto paper sitting sipping espresso on the terrace. Her first attempt at the career she'd really wanted, capturing the soul of a place and showing it in her words to people who might never be lucky enough to visit in person. And even if they did, they wouldn't be there now, experiencing the world through the eyes of a twenty-one-year-old woman, in love for the first time—with a man, with a place, with a feeling—and on the cusp of an incredible life ahead.

Never mind that it hadn't worked out that way. This place, this villa, this landscape… it had taken root in her heart fifteen years ago and right now it felt like it had never let go. Being here again… How could she do it? Would seeing it through her jaded thirty-six-year-old eyes take away the magic she'd experienced there as a young woman? She hoped not. Holding onto those memories was the last bit of magic she had in a grey and dreary world.

She and Erin were the last out of the limo, and Daphne steeled herself against what she'd find out there. Any moment, something new would jar her out of her memories and remind

28 A REUNION IN TUSCANY

her of all the years that had passed since she was last in Tuscany. Something would break the magic. Maybe something that *wasn't* there. For instance, she wasn't going to turn around and see—

Luca Monroe. No, Luca Moretti now.

She blinked, twice, but the image didn't change.

There he was. The man who had made her whole summer magic—and shown her a life that the real world could never live up to.

He was older, of course—they both were. As he stared straight back at her, she could see the fine lines gathering around his eyes— eyes she knew from memory were the exact colour of chocolate gelato. His hair was still fully black, though, curling loosely around his ears, his olive skin a little paler than it had been that summer, as if he hadn't spent as much time out in the sun.

His body had changed, too. She allowed herself only the briefest scan to be sure, swallowing at the breadth of his shoulders now, the lines of muscle hinted at down his torso by his tight T-shirt, and the width of his thighs in his chino shorts.

He'd grown up. Just like she had, she supposed.

She should say something. Did he even recognise her? He was staring, but was that just because he thought she looked familiar and couldn't place her? He wouldn't be expecting to see her here after all, whereas he'd been all she could think about since she'd realised where Erin was taking her.

Maybe he didn't remember her at all. Fifteen years was a long time, and it had only been one summer. One brief, sparkling summer fling.

He'd probably forgotten all about it. She probably should have done, too.

Except how could she when, only a few years after she'd met him, his face had suddenly been everywhere—cookery shows, social media, bookstores… She'd realised quickly that he'd switched to using his mother's maiden name. More authentically Italian to match his cooking, she'd assumed.

But he'd always be Luca Monroe to her.

Her Luca. Her first love.

Why was he here? Even back then, that summer, he'd only been visiting. Villa della Luna had been his friend's family summer home, not his. He'd been on holiday like her.

What were the chances he'd come back to visit at the same time she was here? And did this mean the place hadn't been sold at all?

She broke away from staring at Luca to see their host greeting the rest of their group. He turned to welcome Erin and she realised.

Ben. Luca's friend. He must have inherited the place and turned it into a residential cooking school. It really was just all a horrible coincidence.

Horrible? She glanced back at Luca. Maybe not horrible.

'Erin! And you must be—' Ben broke off, mouth open, glanced back at Luca for a brief moment, and then beamed. 'Daphne Brown. As I live and breathe. I saw your name on the booking form but, I'll confess, I didn't remember your surname. But then, how many Daphnes do you really get to meet? I should have known it was you!'

'Hello, Ben.' Daphne ignored Erin's confused looks and leaned in for the welcome hug he was offering. 'It's good to see you. And, to be honest, I didn't know I was coming here either. Erin booked it all. It's just such a strange coincidence that she booked here...'

'Well, not that much of a coincidence.' Erin shifted from one foot to the other, not looking Daphne in the eye. 'I mean, I knew you'd visited Tuscany after uni, you'd talked about it so much, and I still had the postcards you sent me that summer, so I knew you'd stayed around here and, well, when I found the cooking school I thought it would be perfect. I didn't realise you'd actually know the owner, though.'

'Oh, I don't...' Ben put an arm around her shoulder before she could finish the thought.

'We're *old* friends,' he said. 'And, as it happens, I'm not the only old friend here! Daph, you won't believe it, but look who just stopped by for a visit.'

Oh, God. This was going to be horrible. Even if Luca remembered her, she was pretty sure he wouldn't want to see her again. Not after how she'd left...

'You really don't—'

But it was too late. Ben turned and yelled towards the house, 'Luca! Look who's here to see us!'

CHAPTER TWO

LUCA WINCED AS he heard Ben holler his name. Of course he wanted to talk to Daphne, to re-introduce himself, but he'd really rather not do it in front of an audience. After the way she'd left fifteen years ago he honestly had no idea how their first conversation since might go. He knew he'd had so much he'd wanted to say to her back then—questions he'd wanted answering, accusations he'd wanted to make, things he'd wanted to know... But they'd all flown from his head now, or maybe he'd just stopped caring over the years, because all that mattered now was that she was here.

And the only questions he wanted to ask were, *Did you make the right decision back then? Are you happy now?* Except they didn't really feel like first meeting questions, did they?

The rest of Ben's cohort of students turned as he stepped out of the shadows and into the sunlight, the whispers quickly developing into excited murmurs.

Ben let go of Daphne and stepped to the side to address all the students. 'Everyone, I am delighted to tell you that our co-owner here at Villa della Luna happens to have stopped by for a visit, which means he'll be able to take your first lesson here this afternoon! Luca Moretti, everybody!'

Applause and appreciative calls filled the air, and Luca forced himself to grin and sketch a silly bow in thank you. Before the other students could mob him, though, Ben had grabbed his arm and pulled him towards Daphne and her friend.

'Luca, this is Erin—and of course you remember Daphne.' Ben gave him a little shove towards the women.

'Erin, it's lovely to meet you.' Luca swallowed, and made himself look at Daphne. 'And…it's wonderful to see you again, Daph.'

Across the way, Theo had started taking the other guests off to find their allotted bedrooms, leaving him and Ben alone with Erin and Daphne. Luca couldn't quite decide if that was a good thing or the worst thing ever.

Erin glanced between them in amazement. 'I cannot believe I brought you back to the exact same villa you visited like, what? Fifteen years

34 A REUNION IN TUSCANY

ago? And the same guys are still here? I mean, these are the guys you wrote about in your postcards home, right?'

She'd written to her friend about them? Interesting. Luca watched a rosy blush spread across Daphne's cheeks and wondered what, exactly, she'd said.

'Uh, yes. I met Ben and Luca here when I was working in the village below that summer.' She looked up quickly at Luca and he was surprised to see concern in her eyes. 'I was just explaining to Ben, I didn't know we were coming here. Erin booked it. And, even if I did, I couldn't have known that you'd be here—'

'That's right,' Luca interrupted, before she could work herself up any more about it. 'I didn't even know I was coming myself until last night. It was a, uh, spur-of-the-moment sort of plan.' Necessitated by his ex-girlfriend causing the sort of scene that meant he had paparazzi camping out on the doorstep of his New York home. Again. 'Besides, not many people know I'm part-owner of this place. And anyway, it's not like I expected you to remember me.'

He worked hard at not sounding bitter as he said the last part.

Daphne's eyes widened. 'Really? Because you've been a hard man to miss the past however many years. Ever since that first book of yours hit the bestseller lists, anyway.'

So she'd been following his career? That was interesting.

'I'm surprised you realised it was the same boy you'd met. I mean, I'm not even using the same name.'

'No. Moretti—that's your mother's maiden name, right?' She blushed again. 'I seem to remember you telling me.'

He had. He'd told her that as they'd lain out under the stars one night, talking about their futures, their dreams. He'd told her all about his mother, something he hardly told anybody. And she'd remembered.

Fifteen years and she'd remembered.

That had to mean something, didn't it?

Probably that once she'd walked out and stomped on your heart you got all famous and she's spent the last decade telling people she knew you once. Nothing more than that.

'Anyway, I'm surprised that either of you remember *me,*' Daphne said. 'I mean, I was just one English girl visiting for the summer. You must have met hundreds of girls like me.'

I've never met anyone like you.

The thought flashed through his head before he could stop it, but thankfully he still had enough self-control to stop it coming out of his mouth.

'That was a memorable summer,' he said drily instead, ignoring the flash of memories that threatened to overtake him. The way she'd stood here in this very spot the first day he'd brought her to the villa, shading her eyes as she looked up at the building, a wide smile spreading across her face.

'It's perfect,' she'd murmured, so softly he wasn't even sure she was talking to him. *'It's everything I dreamed of.'*

And he'd thought, *No. You're everything I dreamed of.* And she had been, that whole summer.

Could she be again?

No. She's only here for a few days. She didn't come to see me—didn't even know she was coming here. *I'm not going to let this mean anything.*

It was just one of those weird coincidences that life sometimes threw up, nothing more.

And even if it was…she'd broken his heart fifteen years ago. It wasn't as if he was about to give her another shot at it. Not when it had taken so long for him to recover last time.

'Anyway. It's great to see you again after all these years.' He reached out a hand, his media smile firmly in place, and when she took his fingers in her own he shook them and stepped back. 'I'll let Ben show you where your rooms are. I'm sure I'll see you around this week.'

Some distance. That was all he needed to put this strange interaction back in its box and remember who he was now, instead of the foolish, lovesick boy he'd been at twenty-one.

He made it halfway back towards the safety of the shadows around the villa before Ben called after him, 'Too right, you will. You're teaching their first lesson, remember?'

Erin bounced onto the earthy-coloured bedspread that covered Daphne's allotted double bed. 'Okay, I am going to need the full story here. Clearly, there were some things you left out of your postcards home that summer.'

Technically, they each had their own room for the week, across from each other down a cool, tiled corridor on the first floor of the villa, but Erin had barely dumped her bag in her own room before joining Daphne in hers.

Daphne tried to focus on unpacking, and not the way her heart was still racing after seeing Luca Monroe—no, Moretti—for the first time in fifteen years.

'I wrote about meeting two American-Italian boys who were staying in a family villa just outside the village, right?' Daphne reached into

38 A REUNION IN TUSCANY

her case and pulled out a floaty white sundress to hang up. When she'd packed, she'd definitely imagined more time on the beach, or doing touristy things, and less time cooking. But Erin did always like to have something to *do* on holiday. 'Those were the boys. Ben and Luca.'

'And?' Erin asked impatiently.

Daphne shrugged, and reached for the next dress out of the case. 'And Maria and I—that's the university friend I was staying with, whose family owned the gelato shop and the café in the village, where we were working for spending money—we made friends with them and they let us come use their pool sometimes.'

'I haven't even seen the pool yet,' Erin said. 'The brochure said we were free to use it.'

'It's round the back, down the steps towards the olive grove,' Daphne said without thinking.

Erin grinned. 'You remember this place remarkably well. Think of it often?'

'It was a memorable summer.' She echoed Luca's words flatly. The last thing he'd said before he *shook her hand.* What even was that? Even Ben had pulled her in for a hug. But Ben's arms wrapped around her hadn't made her heart race or her skin tingle half as much as the brief brush of Luca's palm against hers had. That had to mean something, didn't it?

No, she wasn't going to overthink this. He

remembered her. That was enough. Probably he'd put her in the exact same box she'd put him for the last fifteen years—a fond memory from a time when they were barely adults. It was probably embarrassing for him to bump into someone who remembered him from before he was all gorgeous and famous.

Well, before he was famous, anyway. He'd always been gorgeous.

'Okay, but which one did you have the torrid fling with? It was Luca, right? Has to have been Luca.' Erin bounced on the bed a little more in anticipation of her answer.

Daphne concentrated very hard on hanging her olive-green jumpsuit right. 'I never said I had a fling—torrid or otherwise—with either of them.'

'Holiday romance, then,' Erin tried. 'And you definitely did, and you've been hiding it from me—your *best friend*—for actual years, which is possibly a criminal offence, so it's time to fess up. Okay?'

Daphne gave up on the jumpsuit, shoved the hanger into the heavy wooden wardrobe as it was and dropped to sit on the bed beside Erin.

'Okay, fine. I had a thing with Luca that summer. Before he was all famous, obviously.'

'And you never told me! Not even when I

asked Olly for his cook books for Christmas that year!' Erin still sounded outraged.

'It's a little hard to work into conversation,' Daphne replied. *'Ooh, great present, Olly. Did you know I lost my virginity to that guy?'*

'You lost your virginity to him?'

Daphne winced. 'Little louder, Erin. I don't think my mostly deaf father in London quite heard you.' She just really hoped Luca was in another part of the villa.

'I thought you lost it to that creepy guy with the hands at university,' Erin said.

'Bruce?' She pulled a face. 'God, no.'

'You lost your virginity to Luca Moretti. I definitely have to hear this story now.' Erin settled against the headboard, pillows propped up around her, and patted the bed beside her for Daphne to join her.

She sighed. 'Okay, fine. But there's not much more to tell.'

At the time, it had felt like the world's most epic love story. But she had a feeling first love always did.

None of the other sort-of loves that had come since had felt that way. Daphne suspected that was because you only got to have that kind of all-consuming, change-the-world sort of love once. The lucky ones, like Erin and Olly, held onto it, grew up with it and matured into it—

through uni, through new jobs, marriage, kids, and everything else that life threw at them. The rest of the world had to make do with knowing that they'd had it once.

Grown-up love—even for people like Erin and Olly—didn't feel like the fairytale. That wasn't what the real world had to offer, not for ever. Mature, adult relationships were more about practicality and compromise and finding someone you could be comfortable with.

Not someone who made you feel like you had fireflies in your chest.

Or someone who took you for midnight picnics in the olive grove and made your first time so magical under the moonlight that no other man had ever matched up.

'Just start talking, Daphne.'

So she did.

It was easy telling Erin about flirting with Luca when he'd come into the gelato shop one day. How she'd felt like a different person in the sunshine of Italy, someone more exciting than boring old Daphne Brown from London. Maria was a gregarious, social friend—a lot more like Erin than Daphne—who she'd met at university and had invited her out to her family home in Italy for the summer. It had been the first time Daphne had been away from home for so long, and she hadn't been sure her par-

42 A REUNION IN TUSCANY

ents would let her go, but she was twenty-one and they couldn't exactly stop her.

She remembered asking her dad, saying, *'Please. Just let me have this one summer.'*

She'd known even then what the rest of her life would look like if her father got his way. She'd be back working for the family firm, organising print runs and dealing with typos on signage.

But she'd hoped and she'd dreamed that this summer would be the first step to something new, to a career she could love, travelling the world and writing about it so others could experience it through her.

And even if she couldn't have that… She'd wanted one wild summer, and she'd got it.

She told Erin about swimming in natural pools and kissing behind waterfalls, about lying under the stars together in the olive groves, about Luca's motorbike and how they'd explored the countryside together.

'And then I came home and he went on to become a culinary superstar.' She shrugged. 'End of story.'

'Why did you never *tell* me any of this?' Erin demanded.

Daphne tipped her head back against the wall. 'I don't know. I guess…it never felt real, once I was home. It was like a dream I had, or

SOPHIE PEMBROKE

a movie I'd watched. I left it all behind when I left Tuscany and went back to the real world.' Along with her dreams.

Which didn't mean she'd forgotten any of it. Not for a moment.

'But…how did it end? I mean, how did you leave it?' Erin's forehead had creased up in confusion. 'In the movies they always make a plan to meet again in the same spot in two years or something. But you're only here again by accident. So did you break up? Or what?'

She didn't want to tell this part of the story. But she knew her best friend. There was no way Erin would let her get away with anything less than the truth.

'He…he asked me to go with him. He was planning on travelling the country, learning about Italian cookery, before going back to chef school in New York. And he knew I was interested in travel writing, so he thought if we travelled together…it would be an amazing first step for both of us, and we'd get to stay together instead of having to go our separate ways. But I…'

'Your mum.' Erin grabbed her hand. 'Of course. You came home early because she got sick, didn't you? That was the first time, right?'

Daphne nodded. 'It was probably for the best. Not Mum, I mean, but…it was good that

44 A REUNION IN TUSCANY

I had a reason to leave. I mean, it never would have worked out. It was a summer fling! And I'm not exactly the "travel round the country writing and just see what happens" type, am I?'

Erin laughed. 'No. I love you, but no. I couldn't believe you'd even agreed to spend the summer in Italy in the first place! It was totally out of character.'

'I know.' She smiled, remembering the girl she'd been—on the outside at least. 'I felt like a different person that summer. And then it was back down to earth with a bump.'

Back to being the sensible one. The responsible one. The daughter who kept her spoken dreams small, her wishes easy, so she never had to ask for more than anyone could give her.

But inside, she'd dreamt of being so much more. And only Luca had ever known that.

'And how did Luca feel about you leaving?' Erin asked.

'I'm sure he was relieved! The last thing he must have really wanted was me tagging along after him on his big adventure.' Not that she'd exactly asked. She'd just got the phone call and…gone. She'd hadn't even left him a note, just told Maria to explain that she had to go home if he ever showed up and asked.

Erin didn't look convinced. 'Then why did he ask you to go with him?'

SOPHIE PEMBROKE 45

'I don't know. Moonlight and romance. Probably wine—*definitely* wine. He'd have regretted it, I'm sure.' Things would have fallen apart sooner or later, though. They always did. And really, it wasn't as if she was going to actually build her dream life with a holiday fling when she was barely into her twenties, was it? That was just a dream. 'No, everything worked out for the best.'

Even if, coming back to Villa della Luna after so long and seeing Luca again... Daphne couldn't help but imagine another life. One in which she'd made a very different choice—and maybe everything *had* worked out after all.

Thunk. Thunk. Thunk.

The blade of his knife connected heavily with the wooden chopping board—heavier than it should, than he'd teach the students later—as Luca methodically sliced potatoes. It was... therapeutic. Meditative. Something like that. He'd definitely done an interview with some influencer who talked about cooking being a way of getting out of her own head and into the moment.

The only problem was that the moment Luca was dwelling in as he worked was fifteen long years ago.

'Okay, I'm going to need us to revisit what

A REUNION IN TUSCANY

just happened there.' Luca looked up to find Ben in the doorway, leaning against the frame as he watched him work. 'A *handshake*, Luca?'

'It felt appropriate,' he said stiffly. No way he was telling Ben that he'd been afraid that if he'd hugged Daphne out there he wouldn't have wanted to let go. Again.

As angry as he'd been when she'd left, seeing her again...he could still feel that pull between them. That urge to reach out and touch her and make sure that she was real. Still found himself staring at her lips, her eyes, the curve of her shoulder...remembering.

'For a new business acquaintance, perhaps. Not the girl you spent a whole summer mooning over when you were twenty-one.'

'I did not moon.'

'You most definitely did.' With a sigh, Ben came fully into the kitchen and pulled up one of the wooden stools, scraping it across the stone floor as he set it close enough for a more private conversation, even though they were alone.

Oh, God, that meant he was planning a heart-to-heart.

Ben had never been one for getting in touch with his emotions when they were growing up—not least because he came from the sort of family who thought you were better off not having any, and if you *had* to have them, at the least they should never be on *show*. Luca's family had been much the same, so they'd managed their formative years by making jokes about things that mattered and ignoring how it really felt.

But since Ben had fallen in love with Theo—and admitted his sexuality to the world, after long years of chasing women he didn't want just to keep up appearances—he was all about cracking open the heart and letting out all the feelings.

Luca *hated* it. Not least because admitting his feelings had never got him anywhere before.

He'd opened up to Daphne that summer and given her every feeling he had, and look how that had ended up.

'Luca.' Ben gave him that solid, older brother look—the one that said, *We might not be related by blood, and I might technically be six months younger than you, but I've got my life sorted out and you haven't, so you should listen to me.*

Luca had always thought that becoming internationally successful and ridiculously wealthy in his chosen career should have been enough to be able to say he had his life sorted. But apparently not.

'Ben,' he replied, equally solemnly.

48 A REUNION IN TUSCANY

His friend rolled his eyes. 'I'm being serious here.'

'I noticed.'

'I think you need to tell me exactly what happened when Daphne went home that summer.'

Luca froze at the request—no, demand. Ben wasn't asking. He *expected* this information.

Needing a distraction, Luca turned back to his potato slicing, busying himself with the knife and hoping his hands wouldn't shake. 'I told you at the time. She had to go home—I mean, she was only ever here for the summer, right? And I had plans, so I got on with them. I never expected to see her again.' Let alone here and now. Unexpected and blindsided.

Ben was silent, and when Luca gave up on the potatoes, pushing the chopping board aside and turning to look at him, he found his friend watching him carefully.

Finally, Ben spoke. 'We didn't talk about it at the time. We didn't *talk* about things then. But I knew even then it was more than that. You were…broken. And I know a lot of that must have been things with your father, walking away from the family fortune and all that. But some of it was Daphne too, wasn't it?'

Luca looked away. Didn't answer.

He didn't have to.

'I thought that summer it was just a holiday

SOPHIE PEMBROKE

fling. That you were just letting off steam after the row with your father.'

'It was,' Luca said.

Ben ignored him. 'And then she left and you threw yourself into work and building your culinary empire for the next decade and a half, never mentioned her again, never looked back, and never *fell in love*. Then she shows up here and you shake her damn hand like a stranger. So now I'm thinking maybe it was something more.'

'Not everyone meets their soulmate and declares it the same weekend,' Luca pointed out. 'Until you met Theo you were still dating *women,* for heaven's sake. You were so far in denial you hadn't even let yourself date anyone of your preferred gender, and then Theo showed up and your life made sense. Maybe my Theo hasn't shown up yet.'

'Or maybe you're not looking hard enough to see them.' Ben sighed. 'And I *did* date men. I just didn't tell you—or anyone—about it. Until I met Theo…it wasn't worth the hassle of telling my family I was gay.'

That stung. Luca rubbed at his chest as if it had been an actual blow. 'You know you could have told me.'

Ben gave him a weary smile. 'Except we didn't talk about things like feelings back then, did we? I thought we could now, but you're still building up those walls you started after that summer. Hell, they must be a thousand feet high by now. Luca, don't you think it's time you let someone in?'

I let her in.

But that was half a lifetime ago, nearly.

Luca sighed. Maybe Ben was right. Maybe it really was time to talk about this.

'Fine. I fell in love with her that summer. I asked her to go with me when I left and she disappeared back to London faster than I could pack a bag. She broke my heart.' Luca shrugged. 'But…maybe it was for the best. It was what gave me the drive to go out and do what I really wanted with my life. And it's not like I've spent the last fifteen years thinking about her! I have dated women. Like, quite a lot of women really.'

'Yeah, but have you ever loved any of them?' Ben asked with a sad sort of smile.

Luca turned away again. 'None of them have been my Theo. Not yet.'

He was starting to think maybe never.

Ben seemed to sense that the conversation was over—or maybe he just looked at the clock and realised that the students would be gathering soon. Either way, he clapped Luca on the shoulder and headed for the door, pausing when he reached it to look back once more.

'I'm glad you came here this week. I'm even glad that Serena reminded you how much you hate celebrity pseudo relationships and all the drama that comes with them. I think you need some villa time—and a fresh start.' Then he was gone, before Luca had time to think of a response.

Which was probably for the best. He wasn't sure he even had one.

The kitchens at Villa della Luna had obviously been expanded and adapted when Luca and Ben transformed the place into a cookery school. Daphne had vague memories of the previous kitchen as being a dark beamed, shadowy place where they'd raid the freezers for ice for their drinks or grab marshmallows for late-night firepit snacks, but it wasn't somewhere they'd spent a lot of time. Mostly they'd been out in the pool, or on the terrace, or around the firepit in the garden.

Or in Luca's room. Most nights.

Daphne shook away the memories and focused on the kitchens as they were *now*.

The floors were covered in traditional stone tiles, the walls a creamy white, except where classically Tuscan tiles in terracotta, cream

52 A REUNION IN TUSCANY

and olive protected them, and the whole of the large kitchen area was segmented by brick-lined arches. At one end, a huge arched window opened up to the terrace beyond, letting in oodles of glorious Italian light. And in front of it sat a long wooden table with mismatched chairs, capable of sitting at least twenty people. So far, so traditional.

The kitchen equipment, however, seemed state-of-the-art to Daphne's eyes. Yes, there was a traditional range cooker in one alcove, but it looked brand-new. Along one long wall of the space, each student had their own small station to work at, either side of an oven shared between two, with shelves above and below that held everything they'd need for their first lesson.

Daphne would never have described cooking as a hobby, or something she'd do for fun. Her father had liked plain, no-nonsense food and Tommy had been a picky eater when he was young, so meals at home had tended to be basic even before her mother got sick.

Her first experiences of cooking at all had been in school food tech lessons, and then fending for herself at university—neither of which had lent themselves to high quality food over-all. After that, it had been about keeping her father and siblings fed through her mother's illness and, after she was gone, stretching the family budget far enough in the supermarket that everyone got what they needed to keep going.

Food was fuel, and cooking was necessary. She'd never really thought about it beyond that.

Erin, on the other hand, *loved* to cook, to create new meals for her and Olly, and to spend time ambling around farmers' markets sampling goods. She really shouldn't be surprised that she'd chosen one of Villa della Luna's cookery holidays as the destination for their getaway.

Still, sitting at the long wooden table in one of the mismatched chairs, watching as Luca demonstrated the meal they were going to make together for their shared dinner that night, she was starting to see the appeal. The way he talked about the ingredients they were using, where they came from—all local— and how the flavours mixed together to create something magic…he drew her in. And not just her—every other student around the table seemed captivated too.

The only problem was the effort it took to force herself to concentrate on the food, instead of Luca himself. The easy smile he shared with them all as he worked. The way his broad shoulders shifted under his white shirt. His dark hair flopping over his forehead until he shook it back.

She tried to tell herself that she was just remembering the boy she'd known. But as the lesson progressed, she had to admit it wasn't true. She was mesmerised by *this* Luca, the fully matured version. Imagining how he would be now, instead of then. How he'd smile just for her. How he might brush her hair from her face and tuck it behind her ears. How he might kiss...

It only got worse when they moved to their own workstations and he came around to see how they were each getting on and to offer his advice. She managed to mostly ignore him as he helped Erin with her sage leaves, but when he stood behind her to watch over her shoulder, Daphne could feel the heat of him through the thin fabric of her sundress and she promptly forgot everything she ever knew about how to slice potatoes. Or anything at all, really.

'Here.' His hands appeared at her sides, reaching forward to cover her own, and Daphne's breath caught in her chest. 'Like this.'

In a moment, she was cast back to a lakeside fifteen years ago, when Luca had stood behind her, his body against hers and his hands covering her own as he taught her how to skim stones across the placid water. They'd laughed and joked and she'd felt every brush of his skin on hers until it was time to head back to the villa. She'd sat behind him on that motorbike of his, hanging on for dear life and knowing that she'd never felt so alive...

'Do you think you have it, now?' Luca asked, his voice low and warm by her ear, and it took her a moment to remember he was talking about the meal preparation, not skimming stones. She nodded jerkily. But she didn't breathe again until he'd moved on to the next student.

At the end of the session, she and Erin both had edible meals, although Daphne had no idea how.

Standing by the terrace doors, Ben clapped his hands together and grinned. 'Now, we'll take the fruits of our labour out to the terrace and eat!'

This late in the summer, dusk was already gathering. She'd forgotten how late the Italians tended to eat their evening meal. Her father always wanted dinner on the table at six p.m. prompt, and the idea of the meal being a convivial event, drawn out for the pleasure of each other's company, was utterly unfamiliar to him.

But it had been familiar to Daphne once, one summer, and she was surprised how easy it was to fall into it again.

56 A REUNION IN TUSCANY

The terrace around the side of the house from the kitchen held another long wooden table, and it was there they all gathered to eat. Fairy lights were strung along the posts and the roof of the space, along with candles set in olive wood holders dotted along the white tablecloth. The table was decorated with freshly cut rosemary and small twigs of olive leaves, some in small bud vases, other strewn over the tablecloth. And at regular intervals there were carafes of red wine waiting for them—local, Ben assured them.

Daphne felt her heart lighten just looking at it.

Luca took a seat at the opposite end of the table to her and on the other side, which meant that she was able to watch him without being too obvious about it. He made easy conversation with the students around him, throwing his head back with laughter more than once. She tried not to stare at his throat, or remember pressing kisses against the skin there, once.

Erin sat across from her, chatting with Ben at her side and the driver—who turned out to be Ben's fiancé, Theo—on her other. Daphne couldn't quite follow their conversation over the raucous chatter of the rest of the table, but that was fine. She was happy just soaking up the moment.

After they'd eaten the meal they'd made, two of the villa staff brought out a spectacular dessert that they definitely *hadn't* made. Daphne's mouth watered at the sight of the tiramisu, sense memory kicking in as she remembered lying naked in bed with Luca eating the same pudding from glass dishes. He'd fed her spoonsful and stolen kisses between each one, and soon the puddings were abandoned altogether...

This time, when she risked a glance at him, he was already looking at her.

He held her gaze for a long moment, until someone beside him said something to him and he looked away to answer. But Daphne could still feel the heat and the weight of his eyes on her.

She looked down at her dessert and didn't glance down the table again.

Once the meal was over, Ben suggested lighting the firepit down in the gardens and they all wandered down there after him, a motley parade with wine glasses and half empty carafes of wine in hand.

She remembered the firepit from before, but whereas then they'd all sat on the grass around it, now there were designated seating areas— comfy cushioned benches and outdoor beanbag chairs for them to enjoy. Feeling somewhat apart from the conversation, Daphne found herself a seat a little way away from the fire, more secluded than the others, and watched the group from the outskirts, trying to process the day.

The fire cast a strange shadow when someone came to stand beside her, and she looked up to find Theo there. He motioned towards the nearest seat, a universal 'May I sit?' sign, and she nodded.

They sat in silence for a long moment, watching the fire build and listening to the laughter and the chatter of the others. She couldn't even see Luca, didn't know if he'd come out with them or not. Maybe he'd gone back inside. Or home, to his girlfriend or wife. She'd made a point not to keep up with his private life, even as she'd loosely followed his public one. He could have a whole family she didn't know about.

'So, I understand this isn't your first visit to Villa della Luna,' Theo said after a moment. 'Is it as you remembered?'

'Mostly,' Daphne replied. 'And then…not at all.' Every time she thought she remembered it right, something else would throw her off. Like the fancy seating at the firepit, or the way Luca's shoulders seemed to have broadened so much…

'Is it good to be back, though?' Theo asked. And that, at least, was a question she could answer simply. Daphne breathed in the smoky hot air, tipped her head back and closed her eyes, letting the evening wash over her. 'Yes.'

CHAPTER THREE

'ARENʼT YOU WORRIED about that?' Luca waved a hand in the direction of where Theo sat close beside Daphne, obviously both deep in conversation—one that was both amusing and meaningful by turn, if he was judging her facial expressions correctly.

Ben looked up at him in disbelief. 'Worried about what, exactly? That my fiancé—who has never shown interest in a woman once before—is going to fall in love with your ex and elope? Is that seriously what you're thinking watching them?'

'Well, no. Obviously.' Luca shuffled around the hedge a little more to get a better look without Daphne spotting him. 'But she might be telling him all sorts of tales about you when you were twenty-one.'

Ben laughed. 'Honestly? I'm surprised she even remembered me. She only ever had eyes for you that summer.'

And he'd only been able to see her. Same as now.

Teaching that class this afternoon had been unbearable. Every step he demonstrated, he'd felt her watching—and even though his head knew she was only doing it because she was literally there to watch him cook and learn how to do it herself, his body didn't seem to have got the message. Worse still had been helping her with her potato side dish, at her station. What had possessed him to stand behind her and guide her hands, he didn't know—he certainly hadn't done it for any of the other students. But he'd had to keep his lower body angled just enough away that she hadn't been able to feel how much being close to her affected him.

It was ridiculous. She was one woman he'd slept with a few times—okay, fine, a lot of times—fifteen years ago. And yes, maybe his twenty-one-year-old self had imagined himself in love with her. But a lot of time—and a lot of other women—had passed between them since then. Not to mention that she'd made it very clear back then that he'd been nothing more than a holiday fling for her.

It was absurd for him to be so off his game, so unsettled, just because she was here.

If they had been anywhere else, maybe he

wouldn't be so affected. Maybe it was just the villa that was bringing back all those memories. And with the situation with Serena…he was just getting too inside his own head.

Nostalgia, that was all it was. A longing for a past with Daphne that had never really existed. He'd realised over the years that he had to be glorifying it in his memory—their connection, the way she'd seemed to always know what to say, how to touch him for comfort or, well, other things. There was no way any relationship could ever live up to the memory of his time with Daphne that he'd built up in his head since she'd left.

And even that one, perfect relationship he'd imagined had ended badly. Really, he knew better than to rely on love and chemistry for anything any more.

Four more days and Daphne would be gone from his life again. Better to keep his distance and not let this strange reconnection derail his plans, or his head.

Even if he couldn't bring himself to stop watching her, without her knowledge.

She just…drew him in, still. The way her hair hung over her bare shoulder, exposed by the straps of her sundress, like it was waiting for him to push it back. How her smile lit up her whole face. How when she laughed, she laughed with her whole body, shaking with amusement.

How was he supposed to look away from that?

Ben gave him one of his 'looks'—the one that warned he was probably in for another conversation about his feelings if he didn't get it together quick.

'I thought the lesson went well,' Luca said, eager to head that talk off at the pass.

'I suppose.' Ben's 'look' was still going strong. 'If we ignore the fact that you were only performing for one person. The same person you basically cuddled while showing her how to slice potatoes.'

'I did not cuddle her.' If he had, she'd definitely have felt how hard just standing behind her had made him. Damn it, he wasn't twenty-one any more. He couldn't remember the last time the mere presence of a woman had made him feel like that.

Actually, he could. That was part of the problem.

It was only ever her.

'Look, Luca, it's like we were talking about earlier.' Somehow, Ben had lured him into a 'feelings' talk despite his best intentions. 'You need a fresh start. You need to put New York and everything you've been running from behind you and figure out how to be more than just a success. You need to work out how to be *happy.*'

Because in Ben's world, these days, happiness trumped everything else. But somehow Luca was still living in his old world, his father's world. He'd run away that summer to try and do something, be something else, but in the end he'd come full circle. Building restaurants and cultivating fame for success and money wasn't all that much different than building malls and offices for money and status, really, was it?

'Happiness means nothing if you haven't got the money to keep hold of it,' his father had told him, that long-ago summer, when he'd been trying to coax Luca back into the family fold after he'd run off to Italy with Ben.

That conversation had been the first time Luca mentioned his plan of taking to the road to learn how to be the best Italian chef in the world—seeking out the legacy of his late mother's family instead of his father's for a change. He hadn't even told him about Daphne, but his father had still known, somehow.

'There's a girl, isn't there?' He'd sighed wearily. *'Luca, when will you learn? Women are temporary. Success lasts for ever.'*

He hadn't believed him, then. Had fought against it, taking his own path.

And yet, here he was. Still living by those old rules even when he tried not to.

Maybe Ben was right. Maybe he did need a fresh start.

'Okay, say I go with your plan.'

'The Make Luca Happy Again plan, as we'll now be calling it,' Ben interrupted.

Luca ignored him. 'What, exactly, would be my first move, do you think?'

Because happiness seemed a long way away, something over the ocean, something to quest or voyage for. Perhaps Ben was right, and he really was at another turning point in his life. Last time he and Daphne had been together at this villa, he'd blown up his old world and created a new one. Maybe her being here now was his sign that it was time to do the same again.

That didn't mean reliving his youthful romance, or making the same mistakes twice. Just…a poetic sort of symmetry. That was all.

Ben put an arm around Luca's shoulder and manoeuvred him so he was facing Daphne and Theo directly, and without the hedging he'd been hiding behind until now. As if she sensed him there, Daphne looked up at him, her eyes widening even as she nodded along to whatever Theo was saying.

66   A REUNION IN TUSCANY

'First step is to find some closure.' Ben gave him a tiny push in Daphne's direction. 'Go on. Talk to her. You're never going to move on from that summer in your heart if you don't.'

Theo was talking about something to do with the estate, a new project at the villa, she thought, but the moment she'd seen Luca walking towards them Daphne had lost the ability to listen. All she could do was look, watch him getting ever closer, timing his steps with her heartbeats.

Fifteen years. And now they were here.

'And that's why I think the purple hippos will love it,' Theo finished, eyebrows raised as she tore her gaze away from Luca to look at him in confusion, before she realised that he'd noticed her inattention and was teasing her. He patted her on the shoulder. 'I see we have company. I'll leave you two to it.'

'No! You don't have to—' But it was too late. Theo was gone, drifting over towards the firepit, and leaving her at the mercy of her first love.

There were lights hanging from all the trees above, as well as the flickering firelight that warmed and brightened the gardens. Between them, they cast strange shadows, and as Luca reached the place where she was sitting she couldn't quite tell if it was the shadows making him look so…what, exactly? She couldn't make sense of the look on his face, and she froze for a second, unsure if he was about to ask her to leave for good or stay for ever or something somewhere in between.

Be reasonable, Daph. He's probably just come over to say…

Nope. She had nothing. Literally no idea why he'd sought her out or what was about to happen next.

So she waited. And he smiled, and then dropped into the seat Theo had just abandoned, and she let herself relax, just a tiny bit.

'It's still very beautiful here,' she said after a moment, when he stayed silent. 'I like the new seating areas. And the lights.'

Luca glanced around in surprise, and she realised that they wouldn't be new for him. They'd probably been here for ages.

It was only her that was new. Or old. Or both at the same time, however weird that sounded.

'When Ben and I set up the place as a cooking school, we wanted to make it…welcoming, I guess. Somewhere fun to be as well as to learn. And we wanted it to give our students the same feel that a great meal with friends or family does—that sort of never-ending laughter and conversation as well as wine and good food.'

A REUNION IN TUSCANY

As if on cue, a roar of laughter went up from the group by the firepit. From the way Theo was beaming in the middle of it, she imagined it was from something he'd said.

'Well, you definitely seem to have done that.' Daphne flashed him a quick smile, then looked away before she could get too self-conscious. 'How did the cooking school come about?'

Luca glanced over at Ben and smiled. 'Well, Ben's father lost the family fortune in some rather ill-advised business deals—and quite a lot of even more ill-advised gambling, if we're being honest. They were going to have to sell the place. And Ben...he'd struggled, a lot, after we left university. With what he wanted to do, who he wanted to be. And, well, his sexuality I guess now, although I didn't realise that part until he met Theo.'

'I wondered,' she admitted. The summer she'd known him, Ben had fallen 'deeply' in love with at least three different women. She'd never seen him look at a boy, except for Luca, and they'd always been more like brothers than anything else, as far as she could tell.

'Anyway, I'd already had a little bit of success by then, and I had money. Ben didn't want to lose this place, and he needed something to *do*. So we came back here before the villa went on the market, got roaring drunk and… dreamed, I guess.'

He gave a small shrug, along with a half-smile, as if to say, *What else were we going to do?*

'And the school was the dream?' she asked.

He considered his answer far more deeply than she'd expected. 'I think the villa was the dream. That summer we were all here together…that was the last time everything seemed right for Ben, and maybe for me too, in a way. I think we didn't want to let that go so we found a way to keep it. And with my first restaurant just opening and the cookbooks doing so well…it made sense.'

'You did it for Ben.' It wasn't a question, she just knew. 'To make him happy.'

He shrugged again. 'Wouldn't you?'

Daphne looked over at the fire again, where Ben had one arm wrapped tight around Theo's waist and a wide smile on his face. 'It seems to have worked, anyway. Theo's great.'

'He is,' Luca agreed easily. 'And they're good together. Even if figuring out his happy ever after means that Ben wants to talk about our feelings all the time suddenly.' He looked pensive. 'I don't think it's a gay thing, incidentally. I think it's just a happy thing.'

'Happy people always want everyone else to

be happy too,' Daphne agreed. 'I think that's why Erin insisted on bringing me here. Her and her husband, Olly, are…well, I suspect they're a lot like Ben and Theo. Absurdly in love, stupidly well suited for each other, and irritatingly determined to make sure everyone else is just as happy as they are.'

Luca laughed. 'That sounds about right.' Then his expression fell, and Daphne realised too late that she'd said more than she intended to. 'Does that mean you're *not* happy?'

She tucked her feet up under her on the chair and swept the skirt of her dress out over her, to buy time before answering. 'I'm…perfectly content in my life. But I just went through a breakup and, well, Erin thought I needed cheering up. She doesn't get the concept of me being happy on my own.'

Luca watched her for a moment before replying, as if he was waiting for a facade to crack. But it wouldn't, because she was telling the truth. Yes, she'd thought she might be in love with Henry, and that they might have a future together. But her life wasn't about to fall apart because it hadn't happened. She had plenty else going on to focus on.

The same way her life hadn't ended when she had to leave Luca behind. She wasn't the sort to fall apart because of love. Someone had to keep everything ticking over, didn't they?

'That's…good,' he said eventually. 'And I know what you mean. Relationships aren't the be-all and end-all.'

Eager to change the subject, Daphne looked around for another topic of conversation, but she kept coming back to the villa, and the last time they'd been there together.

She leaned back in her seat and studied him. 'The last time I saw you, you'd just told your father you didn't need his money or influence, and you were about to take off and conquer the world alone on that antique of a motorbike. I take it that's what you did?'

His father, as she recalled, was something important in property, absurdly rich, and as determined that Luca would follow in his footsteps as her own father had been that one of his children take over the print shop when he retired.

'More or less.' Luca mirrored her position, twisting to face her as he rested one arm against the back of his seat. 'Definitely the standing up to my father part. I walked out on the family business, my inheritance, everything. Just like I'd told him I would. He was livid, of course, but he couldn't exactly stop me. I wanted to… reconnect with my mother's family again.'

'You hadn't seen them for a few years then, right?' It was funny how his story had stuck in her memory. Daphne remembered lying on a picnic blanket under the stars, surrounded by olive trees, listening to his soft, low voice as he'd told her all about his mother. How she'd been from a loving family here in Italy, before she'd met his father and he'd whisked her away to New York when they were married. How Luca himself had been born in Italy, because she'd been on one last visit to her family when she went into labour early—almost too early. Luca had talked about hazy memories of summer holidays spent visiting the family—always just him and his mom, never his father. Until she'd died when Luca was twelve—cancer, Daphne thought—and the visits had stopped altogether.

'Not since I was twelve,' Luca confirmed. 'Dad…he wouldn't let me see them. I never understood why but…well, my *nonna* says that's what a broken heart can do to a man. Turn them cold.'

'You found your *nonna*, then?' Daphne couldn't help but smile at the thought. Luca had been all alone in the world apart from Ben when she'd known him. She was glad it hadn't stayed that way.

'And my aunt and uncle and my cousins,'

SOPHIE PEMBROKE 73

Luca confirmed. 'They actually run a family restaurant in the village, not far from the gelato café you worked in that summer.'

Daphne gasped. 'Did you know that? When you came here?'

Luca gave a sheepish nod. 'That's *why* we came. I just…hadn't worked up the courage to approach them and tell them who I was, when you were here.'

'That's why you kept coming into the gelato café.' He'd wanted to be close to his family. That made sense.

But he laughed. 'That was why I came into the café the *first* time,' he corrected her. 'After that it was just to see you again.'

A hot flush hit her cheeks and she looked away. 'But you never told me they were there. When we talked about your family…you never said.'

'Because you'd have made me go and see them and I wasn't ready yet,' Luca said bluntly. 'But it all worked out. After you left, I went and introduced myself. Actually stayed there with them and started my training in the trattoria kitchen, before I went out on the road.'

'And then you became a huge star.'

'Not exactly,' he said. 'The first few years after I left the family trattoria were tough. It was hard to leave but… I couldn't learn every-

74 A REUNION IN TUSCANY

thing I needed to there. So then I was working anywhere and everywhere across Italy, mostly for room and board, learning everything I could. Eventually I studied formally in Florence, then back home in New York, working all the time and then… I got lucky.'

'Lucky?' Sounded to Daphne like he'd worked hard for everything he'd got.

'I was in the right place at the right time a lot of the time. Things started to build with my social media accounts, then there was the book deal and the restaurants… I worked hard for it all, I know that. But these things always come down to luck in the end.'

She supposed that was true. 'And your father? You reconnected?'

This time, his smile was more cynical. 'Perhaps unsurprisingly, after spending years telling me I'd never make anything of myself, that I wasn't worth his time or money…once I'd actually found the success and fame I'd worked for, he was interested in being a part of my life again. I… I almost walked away, but he's the only parent I have left. We're in touch again, but I wouldn't say we're close. But I'm back in the will, so I suppose that's something.'

He didn't need the money, Daphne was certain. But maybe he hadn't quite given up hope of a better relationship with his father, one day.

She knew how losing a parent young could change a person's perspective—on everything.

'And what about love?' She hadn't meant to ask the question—it just popped out. She blamed the wine. 'Is there a Mrs Famous Chef back in New York, waiting for you?'

Luca groaned. 'You saw the photos, I take it. Me and Serena rowing outside my restaurant? What am I saying—*everyone* saw them.'

Daphne hadn't, actually, but she didn't mention it. 'Serena's your girlfriend?'

'Was. Is sometimes. But no, I think it's really over this time.' He sighed, and looked up at the stars above them. 'Honestly, romance and love aren't something I really have time for these days anyway. My focus is on my career, and all the incredible opportunities it's given me. For me, dating has pretty much been part of that—most women I date are there to be seen on my arm, or for me to be seen on theirs at events.' He gave a self-deprecating laugh. 'Sorry. That probably sounds awful—I know Ben is horrified by it. But it's kind of the deal with the people I'm around these days, and the women I meet.'

It was awful, she supposed. But at the same time, it made perfect sense to Daphne. In a way, wasn't that what her summer holiday fling with Luca had been about too? She'd listened

76 A REUNION IN TUSCANY

and encouraged him to get out there and follow his dreams—the same as she'd done with Henry, and too many other boyfriends before him. Even if she never quite managed to chase her *own* dreams.

Still, when she remembered how romantic he'd been with her, how tender, it was hard to imagine him shunning love altogether.

'No, I get it. I mean…most of the time it seems to me like everyone is out to get *something* out of a relationship. At least the women you date are upfront about it, and you're not pretending to be offering something that you're not.' Like love. Or a future. Or happiness.

Maybe Erin and Olly—and Ben and Theo—were the odd ones out. The rare, unexpected, real, true loves.

Perhaps it was time for Daphne to grow up and stop believing that she would ever find the same thing. Time for her to take her dreams into her own hands for a change, rather than waiting for permission to chase them.

Except then who would take care of everyone?

She sighed. It was a lovely thought while it lasted, anyway.

Luca frowned as he watched Daphne's expression sink into a dark, contemplative look. What had he said? Was it the idea of transactional relationships that bothered her? No, she'd said she understood that…

Oh. Maybe that was the problem.

'You mentioned…you said you'd just gone through a breakup too?' he asked tentatively. She probably wouldn't want to talk about it—at least not with him. But it felt wrong not to at least give her the opportunity.

They'd always been good at this, talking. For all that Luca tended to avoid talking about his feelings any more than he had to…that one summer, with Daphne, had been the first and only time he'd been comfortable letting it all out. Spilling his secrets and his hopes and dreams and fears.

If he hadn't, he wasn't sure he'd have had the confidence to *actually* walk away from his father and his money and seek his own fortune. It would have been so easy to go back…to take the easy path. But he hadn't.

He had Daphne to thank for that, at least in part. So if she wanted to talk, the least he could do was listen. Even if it did feel a little late now.

She shifted in her seat, pulling on a light cardigan over the dress she was wearing—the one that swirled around her calves when she walked, that had mesmerised him when they'd been walking down to the garden.

'Yes. Uh, Henry. We'd been together…about eighteen months, I suppose.' She shrugged. 'It was probably for the best. We met when he was newly divorced and had just been made redundant. I…well, I hope I helped him get back on his feet, find his confidence again. A little too well, in fact. When he left me, he told me he wanted to go off and seek his true purpose and happiness in life.' She looked up, her gaze meeting his so sharply that he sucked in a breath that stung his lungs. 'A bit like you, I suppose.'

Except *he* hadn't left her. He'd asked her to go with him.

She was the one who had walked away.

'Eighteen months. That's… What about before him? Did you ever get married? Have kids? And what about work? You wanted to be a travel writer. Tell me all about all the places you've been! I want to hear about your life. What has Daphne Brown spent the last fifteen years doing?'

She looked taken aback at his sudden interest. 'Oh, uh, well, not much, I suppose. Or rather, what was expected of me, perhaps. I went home, started work in the family business as my father wanted. Um, it didn't leave a lot of time for travelling. Or writing. My mother… she died a few years later, so I took on more responsibility, keeping the family going. My siblings were both quite a lot younger than me, so…my dad needed me around.'

The family business. He couldn't remember what it was, exactly, but he knew she hadn't been excited about it back then. She'd hoped to escape, to go *everywhere* and bring it home to people through her words. She'd planned to find her passion, as he had. Just not with him.

He felt a pang in his chest at the idea that, while he'd followed through on their dreams, she'd been trapped in the life she'd spent that whole summer hoping to avoid. She looked smaller as she said it, her smile forced and a little sad. It made him want to reach out for her, to light the spark again that he'd seen in her that summer.

'And no, I've never been married. No kids. Just…a lot of boyfriends I thought might be the one who turned out to have bigger dreams than marrying me.' She shrugged. 'Same old, same old.'

She'd settled into a pattern, Luca realised— and one he might even have started. She'd helped him articulate what he really wanted out of life and then given him the confidence to go after it, even if she hadn't been willing to go with him. And it sounded to him like she'd

A REUNION IN TUSCANY

been doing that for boyfriends ever since—building them up and then letting them go.

But it didn't seem like anyone had been doing that for her, not since she'd left Italy fifteen years ago, anyway.

Maybe that was something he could change. In a way, he owed a lot of his success to Daphne—without her push and her belief in him, he might never have had the courage to go after what he really wanted from life.

Now, perhaps it was his turn to do the same for her.

Ben had talked about closure and a fresh start—and this could be it. A chance to pay it forward, to give Daphne what she needed to find the life she wanted. Then, maybe he'd be free of the memories of her, of everything he'd hoped they could be, once.

Even if the attraction between them seemed as strong as ever. They'd moved closer together while they talked. He hadn't even realised they were doing it, but now his knee brushed up against hers, and his hand rested against the fabric of her skirt. It would take almost nothing to lean into her, to brush his lips against her skin…

Luca blinked, and realised his other hand was reaching to tuck a curl behind her ear. He jerked it back quickly, but not fast enough that Daphne didn't notice it too.

'Oh!' Daphne suddenly straightened in her chair, leaning back out of reach.

'Sorry, I—'

'No! I just… Listen.' Suddenly, the gardens around them were quiet. Too quiet. 'I think the others must have all gone to bed.'

He glanced up towards the terrace and saw Ben and Theo heading in, arms around each other's waist. 'Looks like.'

She was on her feet in a moment, before he could find any excuse to drag the moment out longer. 'I should go, too. Early start tomorrow. And heaven knows I need to be well rested to have any hope of cooking whatever you and Ben have planned for us.'

'You'll be fine,' he assured her. 'Daph—'

But she was already moving away, that damn skirt swirling around her calves in a way that made him long to bunch it up in his hands, drag it slowly up her thighs and pull her to him…

'Daphne?' he called again.

This time, she paused and turned back towards him, silhouetted against the villa with the moonlight behind her. And for a moment it could be fifteen years ago all over again and she could be dancing up towards the villa, leaving him to chase her, to catch her, to sweep her up in his arms and carry her to bed...

'Yes?' she said, and he forced himself back into the here and now.

'I'm... I'm happy you're here. That we get to see each other again this week.' It felt at once too little and too much. But it was true.

'I'm happy you're here too,' she replied softly. 'I don't think I could manage being at Villa della Luna if you weren't here too.'

Her words caught him in the chest and he sucked in a breath as he tried to respond. He took a step forward, one hand reaching out for her—

But she was gone. She'd turned away before he'd even moved.

Luca watched her walk all the way back to the villa, remembering once more another night in these gardens, another sundress, another Daphne—a night that had ended very differently.

Then he sighed to himself and dragged himself off to bed too. Daphne was right. They had an early start, and a long day planned.

And despite the impromptu nature of his visit, Luca didn't plan to miss any of it. After all, he had work to do here now.

He had to save Daphne from her own mediocre life before he could move on with his own.

CHAPTER FOUR

DESPITE HER GOOD INTENTIONS, Daphne found herself lying awake long into the night, reliving those moments with Luca in the garden. It had just been so easy to fall back into the same sort of conversation they'd had the summer they'd met. Shouldn't it have been stilted? Awkward? Like that first terrible handshake outside the villa had been.

Maybe it was the wine, or the moonlight, the shadows making it easier to forget the passage of time perhaps. But there were moments when she'd really thought he was going to reach out for her—to touch her, even kiss her…

But then she reminded herself who she was now—and, more importantly, who *he* was—and how much had changed. There was a chance it was all in her head, the villa bringing out her romantic notions again.

Except she recognised that look in his eyes in the moonlight…and he *had* said he was happy

84 A REUNION IN TUSCANY

she was there. That had to mean something, didn't it?

But did she want it to?

With a groan, she turned her pillow over to the cool side, shoved it back under her head and tried to sleep, only to find herself going back over the whole evening again from the beginning in her head.

Daphne yawned all through breakfast—taken out on the terrace again, with juice in the carafes in place of wine—and the morning's cookery lesson. By the end of it, she managed to create some just about edible stuffed pasta, which was just as well, as they were all eating their morning's work for lunch.

'How are they?' Theo asked as he leaned over her shoulder while she ate.

'I've had worse,' she said honestly. 'But I've definitely also had better.'

Theo laughed and clapped her on the shoulder. 'Don't worry. You're in for a *feast* this afternoon—and into this evening—so you don't want to ruin your appetite, anyway.'

When he moved on, Erin leaned in closer. 'Of course, if you hadn't spent the whole morning watching the door for a certain dark-haired chef of your acquaintance, maybe your tortellini would have turned out better.'

'I don't know what you're talking about,'

Daphne lied. Because she *had* been looking for Luca all morning, but there'd been no sign of him.

'And *I* don't know what you and he were talking about last night until after all the rest of us had gone to bed,' Erin said. 'Because you haven't told me. Which is definitely against the best friend code, somehow.'

Daphne shrugged and speared another tortellini on her fork. 'We were just catching up. You know, what we've both been up to over the last fifteen years.'

'That must have been…interesting.' Erin's eyes were wide. 'What did he say?'

'Oh, you know. Wild success, more money than God, women falling at his feet, that sort of thing.'

'Right. And what did *you* say?'

'Just the truth,' Daphne replied. 'That I went home from Italy, took the job in the family business and never looked back.'

Except she had—looked back, that was. She'd spent fifteen years remembering that summer and wondering if she'd ever get to feel that way again. Maybe now she could. If Luca ever reappeared.

Don't be ridiculous. He's been dating actresses and models. He's not going to be interested in me these days.

86 A REUNION IN TUSCANY

The voice in her head was convincing, but she'd seen the way he'd looked at her the night before. Remembered him looking that way back then, too. Maybe she wasn't the sort of woman he was used to now, but that didn't mean he wouldn't consider one last fling for old times' sake, did it?

Okay, now I'm losing my mind. Thinking I could seduce Luca Moretti for...what? Closure?

Even if she succeeded, what difference would it really make? She'd be back in London and back to her old boring life at the end of the week either way.

Another reason to give it a shot...

Erin looked concerned, so Daphne flashed her a happy smile and turned her attention to the top of the table, where Ben was standing, waiting for them all to quieten down.

'Right! As you'll know, if you've been reading your itineraries, this afternoon we're leaving the villa for a little adventure!' Ben beamed as excited chatter started up again.

Daphne glared at Erin. *She* hadn't even seen an itinerary. What on earth had her friend got her into now?

'Don't get too excited,' Ben said with a laugh. 'It's still food-related. We're going to take a little road trip to a village not too far away, where there is a classic Tuscan trattoria run by the people who first taught me—and Luca Moretti, for that matter—to cook. We're going to see how they operate, maybe even help out in the kitchen a little bit—and stay for dinner, of course! So, you've got thirty minutes to freshen up and gather your things and then we're hitting the road. Meet out front of the villa!'

Daphne scrambled to her feet, mind already spinning. The place where Luca had learned to cook? That had to be his family's restaurant, right?

She couldn't help but wonder what stories about Luca the people there might have to tell...

Thirty minutes later—well, forty-five, but only Ben was counting—they were all en route to the village. They'd foregone the limo this time and were piled into two large four-by-fours instead, for the sake of the village streets, Theo had explained. As they arrived in the village, Daphne felt that even the four-by-fours were optimistic—they were wide enough to take up both sides of the narrow roads in places.

She felt a familiar peace settle over her, though, as they climbed out of the cars and experienced the village for the first time. The gelato café she'd worked in that summer was gone, but it had been replaced by another one similar enough to bring back more fond memories. The warm stone buildings, the bright red flowers and lush greenery overflowing from window boxes and planters on metal balconies, the warm air and the brown and green hills in the distance under the bright blue sky...

If she let everything else go, she could really believe she was twenty-one again, waiting for night to fall and the lanterns to come on, and for Luca and Ben to arrive and whisk her and Maria off to some bar or club, or back up to the villa for a moonlight swim.

Ben led them down a winding passage, Theo bringing up the rear to ensure that none of them got lost, and soon they were all filing into a tiny restaurant under a small yellow sign reading 'Moretti's'. The tables were all scrubbed wood, the floor the same stone slabs as up at the villa and the window shutters were thrown open to let in as much light as possible to the small building.

Daphne loved it.

'They close for one afternoon a week to fit us in, every time we have a class running,' Theo murmured from beside her. 'We're lucky to have the connection.'

A balding man with a wide paunch and a

wider smiler met them by the kitchen, along with a petite woman with a thin face and dark hair he introduced as his wife. Luca's aunt and uncle, she supposed. There were handshakes and welcomes and coffees for everyone, and seemingly no rush to get started. Luca's uncle and aunt answered questions about the restaurant, and how long they'd been in business—'For ever!'—and myriad other things before the coffee was done.

Then Luca's uncle clapped his hands together and announced the main purpose of their afternoon.

'And now—you shall learn how to make pizza like an Italian!'

Despite Luca's best plans to make himself part of Daphne's new Italian renaissance—and hopefully lead her to the life she'd wanted before the real world got in the way—he did still have a business to run. As his manager reminded him the following morning, when he woke him up by calling obnoxiously early to remind him about a video call with some investors that Luca had, quite honestly, forgotten existed since he'd arrived home in Italy.

Home. As he quickly showered and readied himself for the meeting, he couldn't help but dwell on the fact that Italy had become home

A REUNION IN TUSCANY

again so fast. He'd travelled and lived all over the world, but in his head he always assumed that New York was home, since that was where he'd grown up, and where he'd gravitated back to after his successes. Having the hottest restaurant in the city that never sleeps, his home town, had been the icing on the cake of his career so far.

So why did Italy still feel so much more like the place that he belonged?

He pushed the thought away to consider later as he took the meeting, said what he hoped were the right things and nodded in probably all the right places. His manager—a terrifying woman called Matilda, who was at least a decade older than him and ran his life and work with astonishing ease—hadn't glared at him anyway, so he supposed he was doing okay.

'When are you coming back?' she asked bluntly once the investors had logged off the call. 'I have paperwork for you. And other meetings to set up.'

'Can't I do them from here?' Luca asked.

Matilda paused in shuffling her papers and looked directly down the webcam at him. 'You can. We have the technology, as they say. I just wasn't aware that you were planning to stay in Italy long enough to make it necessary.'

Because he hadn't told her he was even going until he was already on the plane.

'If you're concerned about the incident outside the restaurant last week, you'll be pleased to know that the gossip rags have already moved on to covering Serena stepping out with her latest co-star.'

Luca winced. 'No, really, Matilda. Don't coddle me. No need to spare my feelings.'

Matilda rolled her eyes. 'You didn't love her. You're not heartbroken. Now stop sulking in Italy and come back to New York and run your business, please.'

'Isn't that what I pay you for?' he joked.

'I rather doubt your fans and customers would be happy with me appearing as you at your next book signing,' she replied drily.

'Good point.' Luca sighed. 'I'll be back soon, I promise. I just have some…stuff I have to do here first.'

'Family stuff?' Matilda's eyebrows were raised in unusual—for her—curiosity.

Luca thought about where Daphne was right now, and how he was missing his aunt and uncle teaching her how to make pizza. 'Yeah, you could say that.'

By the time he made it over to the village where his mother had grown up, and the res-

92 A REUNION IN TUSCANY

taurant his family had run since the beginning of time—according to them—the afternoon was well underway. He slipped in through the back door to the kitchens and watched as dough was kneaded and spun and sauce splattered and mozzarella scattered.

Really, though, he was only watching one person.

Daphne and Erin had collapsed into giggles at their counter, over something to do with one of their pizzas, he assumed. Daphne had flour in her dark hair and her cheeks were pink, her eyes bright. For the first time since she'd reappeared in his life, she looked entirely like the girl he used to know. Brimming with life.

'Having fun?' he asked, leaning against the counter, out of the flour danger zone.

'Lots, thank you,' Daphne replied. Erin, he noticed, faded away towards some of the other students, flashing Daphne a knowing look as she went. A clever woman, Erin, obviously. 'You didn't tell me last night we'd get to visit your family restaurant.'

'I thought it would be a nice surprise.' Despite the risk of ruining his clothes in the pizza carnage, Luca couldn't resist moving closer to Daphne. 'I'm glad you got to see it, though. If you'd stayed…well. If you'd been here when I finally found the guts to introduce myself to my own family, you'd have experienced it all long ago.'

She didn't seem offended at his mention of how things had ended between them, at least.

'Meeting the people who taught Luca Moretti to cook, though…quite the honour.' She wiped her hands on a tea towel. 'I'm not sure I'm doing this kitchen justice, though.'

'I'm sure it'll be delicious.' Damn it, he'd moved closer again. When had that happened? And what was he planning to say next? He couldn't remember, because Daphne was standing right in front of him, eyes wide, flour in her hair, and all he could think was how easy it would be to kiss her, to lift her up onto the counter…

'Luca! You made it at last. Your aunt and uncle were beginning to despair of you.' The words, spoken in a slightly creaky voice and all in Italian, were accompanied by a smack on the arm.

'Nonna.' Luca pushed all inappropriate thoughts about Daphne from his mind and turned to embrace his grandmother. It felt as if he had to lean down even further than last time to reach his arms around her. 'I missed you.'

'Why, have you been gone?' The old woman arched her eyebrows mischievously. 'I didn't

94 A REUNION IN TUSCANY

notice. Now, come and sit with me and we will tell each other everything we have missed.'

He flashed Daphne an apologetic look, but nobody denied Nonna when she wanted to talk. She led him through to the restaurant proper, closed to patrons for the afternoon, and they settled at her usual table—before she sent him off again to fix her drink and bring her olives and other snacks. Luca caught Daphne's gaze on him for a moment as he passed near the kitchen door, but didn't stop. As much as he wanted to speak with her again, if Nonna saw him paying any extra attention at all to a woman, that would be it. She'd have married them off by sunset. He was probably in enough trouble on that front as it was.

'Here you are, Nonna.' Luca dropped back into his seat, mission accomplished, and smiled at his grandmother. 'Now, what's been going on around here?'

'Oh! Let me tell you…'

It was easy to let the rapid flow of Italian run over him as his grandmother regaled him with tales of the local dramas and scandals—all hugely exaggerated, he was certain. Nonna had a flair for storytelling and she never let the truth get in the way of it.

She'd been the first one to welcome him when he'd shown up on the doorstep with nothing but a photo of his mother in his hand. The first to recognise him, to bring him in and tell the uncle and aunt he'd never met before that he'd be staying. She'd taught him to love food in ways he'd never thought of before. And she'd told him stories of his mother that he'd never heard—and never would have heard if his father had got his way.

'And what about you?' Nonna had a gleam in her eye that made him slightly anxious. 'What has brought you home so unexpectedly?'

'He had a row with his girlfriend, Nonna.' Ben arrived just in time to humiliate him fully. Excellent.

'You know she's not actually your *nonna*, right?' Luca asked.

Ben shrugged, then bent to kiss Nonna on the cheek. 'I'm here more than you. She likes me best now.'

'Now, now.' Nonna patted Ben's hand. 'I don't have favourites.'

'But you should! I'm the only one who is actually your grandchild!' Luca objected, holding back his laughter.

'Is that so? It's been so long since you visited that I forget...'

Ben roared with laughter at that, bringing Theo over to find out what was so funny, and soon everyone else had joined them too. The

96   A REUNION IN TUSCANY

pizzas, apparently, were being cooked by Luca's uncle, who was unwilling to give up his pizza oven to mere students, and the rest of them were to take seats at the long table that had been set out along the middle of the restaurant for them.

Luca didn't know if it was chance, design or the machinations of his friends or hers, but he was barely even surprised when he took the last seat at the table—and realised he was seated next to Nonna, with Daphne on her other side. And Nonna was already looking like she was ready to cause trouble.

Well. This would either go incredibly well or incredibly badly.

Luca's *nonna* was an absolute hoot.

Sitting beside her while they all devoured the pizzas they'd made, Daphne was very aware that Luca was listening in to everything they were saying from further along the table. That didn't stop Nonna telling all the most embarrassing tales she could about Luca from his visits with his mother as a child, though—from his first taste of gelato to the time he sat down in the middle of a pizza, nappy and all. From what she could tell in the candlelight, Luca was blushing, but he made no move to stop her talking.

Daphne supposed that, with his mother gone,

his *nonna*, aunt and uncle were the only people who remembered those early days, when she'd have brought him here to see their family. After her death, his father had cut them off completely.

All of the stories were about Luca as a baby or toddler, or at most as a child, because that was the only time they'd known him, until he was an adult.

'As much as I'm loving the embarrassing stories about Luca,' Theo said, leaning across the table, 'I want to hear more about your latest marriage success, Nonna!'

'Marriage success?' Daphne asked. Had Luca's grandmother got remarried?

'Ah, yes.' Nonna leaned back in her chair with her arms folded across her chest and a smug smile on her face. 'Darling Lucia and Alessandro. They were married last weekend, just as I predicted! There'll be a baby within the year, you mark my words.'

Daphne cast a confused look Luca's way, and he explained for the sake of the whole table.

'Nonna has a very special talent. Matchmaking.' When everyone laughed, he went on. 'No, no, it's really quite serious. She's responsible for well over half the marriages that have taken place in this village over the last fifty plus years.'

98 A REUNION IN TUSCANY

'It's true,' Luca's Aunt Rosa said. 'Girls come to her when they're looking to meet their soul mate. Boys usually when they're too scared to ask a girl out and need Nonna to tell them it's all going to work out.'

'And sometimes she just gets in there and gives people a push before they even realise they need one,' Ben said. From the way he was looking lovingly at Theo, Daphne suspected that Nonna had been involved in their getting together, too.

'How do you do it?' Daphne asked. 'I mean, how can you tell?' Because, really, if someone in London had that kind of ability it could have saved her from all kinds of dead-end relationships.

Nonna took her hand between the two of hers, patting it gently. 'Sometimes it's in the eyes, the way they watch a person move around the room. Sometimes it's how they don't look at them at all, like it's too painful. But mostly… it's just another sense—like sight or scent. I just sense love in the room, and I know.'

Daphne kept her gaze firmly on Nonna's hands. Just in case.

'Of course, she's never managed to match up our Luca here,' his uncle Rocco said with a laugh. 'He's far too wily. Never brings a girl home with him, just in case.'

'Maybe that's why he's come home now,' Aunt Rosa said, a sly smile on her face. 'After his latest relationship implosion, maybe he's ready to trust Nonna at last.'

'That's not—' Luca started, but Uncle Rocco cut him off.

'Yes! Because remember, when he came home the first time, after all those years his father kept him from us? Wasn't he heartbroken that summer, too?'

'Oh, he was so miserable!' Rosa laughed fondly. 'Life wasn't worth living without that girl—whoever she was, he certainly never brought her here. But she was the *most* beautiful, the *most* wonderful and he'd never meet anyone like her ever again—even though he'd only known her for a month at most before she left!'

'Ah, young love,' Rocco said mockingly. 'Puppy love!'

Daphne stared very, very hard at the table and hoped her cheeks weren't too red. Either Luca's aunt and uncle were talking about *her,* or Luca had fallen in love every other week that summer and she was—as she'd suspected—only one in a long line of women. She wasn't sure which was worse.

Either way, she wasn't going to risk looking at Luca or Ben for confirmation.

100 A REUNION IN TUSCANY

'I was twenty-one,' Luca said quietly. 'How old were you two when you got married again?'

'That's not the point,' Rosa said, which Daphne took to mean they hadn't been much older than twenty-one at the time. 'The point is, are you finally ready to let Nonna match you up with a *real* woman—someone you might actually love and marry?'

Daphne's heart seemed to stall in her chest at the idea. And then Nonna squeezed her hands and let go, and she almost fell off her chair. God, this was uncomfortable.

'I think Luca is the sort of man who needs to find love for himself,' Nonna said sagely. 'It's the only way he'll ever believe in it. I have my talents, but some cases are beyond even me!'

Everyone laughed, as Luca wrapped an arm around Nonna's shoulders and hugged her close. Daphne looked up at last, hoping it was safe, only to find Ben and Theo both watching her carefully, a clear message in their shared gaze.

See what you did to him?

When she jerked away she found herself looking straight at Luca, which was no better. His own unspoken message was more oblique, she couldn't read it in the candlelight. But he had one, that was for sure.

Daphne didn't understand. She'd never imagined Luca had wasted any time thinking about her after she'd left Italy that summer. He'd been too busy building his cooking empire and his incredible life, surely? But if what his family said was true, and about her…

She realised, suddenly, that their heart-to-heart the night before had been woefully incomplete. They'd talked about their lives since they'd parted, sure—covered the last fifteen years of his successes and her failures.

But they'd never covered this: the days and weeks immediately after they'd parted.

Maybe they needed to. Maybe this week could really close that chapter of their lives—and maybe she'd finally be able to move on properly afterwards.

She hoped.

Luca wasn't sure that having his family roast him over a long-ago heartbreak in front of the woman who'd actually *broken* his heart was exactly anyone's idea of a good night, but he could never regret spending time with Nonna and his aunt and uncle. Seeing Daphne there too, whispering with Nonna while his grandmother held her hands in her own wrinkled ones…it had tugged at his heart as an image of what might have been, long before Rosa and Rocco had started reminiscing.

A REUNION IN TUSCANY

He wondered if Daphne had realised they were talking about her. Maybe she hadn't. There'd been a lot of wine with dinner. There was still a chance. He hoped.

And at least Nonna hadn't decided to try and set him up with anyone while he was there. He couldn't think of many things more awkward—especially if she'd chosen Daphne and they'd had to explain their history.

Except she wouldn't have chosen Daphne, would she? Because Nonna's love predictions were always right and he already knew that Daphne wasn't the one for him. Otherwise, she never would have walked away the first time he'd asked her to stay.

As the evening drew to an end the group piled out of the restaurant waving tipsy goodbyes and loaded back into the cars, their designated drivers—Ben and Theo—behind the wheels. Except, of course, there was no room for Luca, since he'd been dropped down earlier by one of the staff on their way home, after his phone calls and meetings had finished.

'Don't worry, I'm happy to walk,' he told Ben when his friend offered to come back for him. 'It's not so far. We used to do it all the time when we were younger, remember?'

While the twisty road systems and direction of the villa's driveway made it a fifteen or twenty-minute drive, if he crossed straight over the fields it was only a two-mile walk.

'We're not twenty-one any more, thankfully,' Ben replied with a laugh. 'But if you're sure.'

'I am.' The walk would do him good. Help him clear his head. And, if he was lucky, by the time he'd got back Daphne would have gone to bed and he could avoid any awkward questions she was planning to ask him.

'Okay, then.' Ben got into the car and gave Theo in the other vehicle the signal to leave.

It was only then that the door to the restaurant opened and Daphne came tumbling out.

'Hell, did they leave without you?' Luca reached for his phone to call them back, but Daphne shook her head.

'I figured you'd be walking, so I told them I'd keep you company. We used to do it all the time, right?' Since he'd just used the same argument, Luca didn't even bother trying to disagree with her.

She was swaying ever so slightly so he knew the wine had got to her, but there was a stubborn, determined look in her eye that told him she was going to get her own way tonight— whatever that turned out to be.

'Right.' He sighed, and shoved his phone back in his pocket. 'I suppose we'd better get walking, then.' He angled his arm towards her, and she took him, leaning against his shoulder just a touch as they made their way across the village square.

'It was nice to meet your family,' Daphne said after a while. 'Since, you know. I left before I could.'

'Right.' So, were they talking about this? Surely that wasn't a good idea when they were both tipsy and stuck with each other in the dark for the next couple of miles? Probably better to change the subject. 'Did I tell you what happened when I did go introduce myself to them for the first time?'

'No. What?' She looked up at him with wide, curious eyes and he knew his distraction had worked.

He smiled, remembering the day he'd finally shown up at their restaurant ready to tell them who he was, when his *nonna* had taken one look at him and said, *'It took you long enough. We were starting to think it would be winter before you came in here.'*

'Turned out they knew who I was all along,' he said. 'They were just waiting for me to invite myself in.'

'I'm glad you found them again.' There was something wistful in Daphne's voice. 'Glad that you had them, after your father cut you off.'

'They've been more family than he ever

was,' Luca admitted. Maybe he'd had more wine than he'd thought, because he wasn't usually this honest or open.

Or maybe it was just that it was Daphne. Fifteen years apart, and he still hadn't broken the habit of opening up to her.

He didn't know what that meant. Wasn't sure he wanted to.

They made it out of the village and halfway through the nearest field before she asked the question he'd known was inevitable since the moment they'd started walking. Distractions could only do so much, after all.

'Were they…they were talking about me, weren't they? Your aunt and uncle, at dinner? The girl who—' She cut herself off, so Luca finished for her.

'The girl who broke my heart?' He sighed. 'Yeah, Daph. They were talking about you.'

As if it could have been anyone else. That whole summer, he hadn't been able to look at another girl. When Daphne was there, she'd been his sun, his moon, his only light.

Of course they'd been talking about her.

'I didn't… I didn't realise.' Her voice was soft, and she gripped his arm just a little bit tighter. 'I figured…you had all these big plans. I thought you were going to go out there and conquer the world—exactly like you did. I figured I'd only ever have got in your way, that you'd probably regretted asking me to go with you before I even left. I thought… I thought you'd be relieved that I'd gone.'

Her words struck him in the chest like rocks. 'Why…what on earth could make you think that?'

Had she really not known how he'd felt? How besotted he'd been?

Luca was a realist, and he knew full well that the chances that they'd have really made it at twenty-one were slim. Odds were good that they'd have fallen out somewhere along the line, and she'd have gone home to her family then. He could admit that now.

But then? If anyone had asked him back then he'd have sworn up, down and blind that they were for ever. That was why his heart had hurt so much.

'I just…maybe I just figured that was who you were,' she said finally, and Luca couldn't shake the feeling that she'd almost said something else. 'A guy who knew how to live life to the fullest, and who was going to get out there and make the world do exactly what he wanted it to do. And a guy like that didn't need me hanging off his coat tails, holding him back.'

'I see.' The worst part was, she was probably right. If she'd stayed…would he really have achieved everything he had over the past fifteen years? Chances were, he'd have settled down in the first place he found and made sure he was home every night to take her to bed. He'd been running away from the feeling of losing her for so long, it was hard to imagine how different his life would have been if she'd stayed.

He honestly didn't know if it would have been worse or better.

But back then...*she'd* wanted that too. She'd wanted to travel, to have adventures, to see the world and write about it. He'd wondered if she'd thought he would hold *her* back, except she hadn't done any of those things. As far as he could tell, she hadn't even tried.

They walked the rest of the way across the fields in silence, until they came to the side gate that led to the villa's estate. The gardens were quiet, so he assumed everyone else had gone to bed. They should too; they had another big day planned tomorrow, exploring the nearby vineyards and doing a wine-tasting. It should be a good day.

As they reached the terrace he turned to tell Daphne goodnight, carefully detangling his arm from hers. But, to his surprise, she grabbed his sleeve before he could leave and when he turned back to face her she was looking up at him with wide eyes that seemed to glow in the moonlight.

'Luca…who did you think I was? Back then?' She bit down on her lower lip as she waited for his answer.

He could kiss her, he realised. Right now. They were standing so close, their voices little more than a whisper between them, that he could just dip his head and take her lips in his in a moment.

God, he wanted to. He wanted to feel her mouth on his again. Wanted to reach his hands around her waist and pull her close, hold her body tight against him…

But she was still waiting for his answer.

He'd thought she was so many things, back then. Had believed she could be anything she wanted to be—the same way she'd convinced him he could be. But those weren't the words that bubbled to the surface of his mind as she asked her question.

Maybe it was the moonlight, or the wine, or his *nonna*'s influence, or even just the way his body tightened at the sight of her teeth pressing into her lip…but Luca answered honestly, even knowing he'd regret it in the morning.

'Daphne, I thought you were my for ever.'

Her small gasp echoed through the night,

and her hand tightened on his forearm before he could even think of running away.

'For ever?' she breathed.

He nodded. 'For ever.'

She was so close now he could see when she swallowed, her throat bobbing. Could watch as her eyes fluttered closed. And he knew, in his gut, that if he leaned in and kissed her now, she'd let him.

He could kiss Daphne Brown one more time.

But then what?

He didn't want that kiss just for the sake of nostalgia, because they were both reliving their past. He didn't want a sad memory kiss.

Because, he realised suddenly, he didn't want to kiss the memory of Daphne at all. He wanted to kiss *this* Daphne, the grown woman he'd only known for a couple of days. The woman who hadn't lived the life he'd expected for her, who hadn't left without a word for any of the reasons he'd imagined.

The woman, he realised now, he hadn't begun to understand fifteen years ago, even though he'd thought he knew her better than anyone when they were together.

If he kissed her now, when they were tipsy and maudlin about the past...he might never understand her at all.

And he wanted to.

110   A REUNION IN TUSCANY

He wanted to kiss her when he knew it all. Her whole story. And that wasn't going to happen tonight. It was too late and they were too tired. And he couldn't shake the feeling that she was still hiding something from him.

So instead, he peeled her fingers from his arm, pressed his lips to her forehead in a sweet goodnight, then turned away and went to bed.

He wouldn't kiss Daphne Brown tonight. But tomorrow...if she opened up to him the way he hoped she would, tomorrow was fair game.

CHAPTER FIVE

'YOU LOOK LIKE you need this.'

Daphne took the travel mug of coffee from Theo gratefully as they all climbed aboard the four-by-fours the following morning for their next adventure. Peeling back the lid, she saw that the coffee was strong, black and hot. Perfect.

'Thank you,' she said with feeling.

Theo smiled, leaning against the car as he looked at her. 'Bad night's sleep?'

'Something like that.' She hurried past and into the car before he could question her any further.

Because the truth was, she didn't think she'd slept at all. And not for any of the reasons she suspected Theo was whispering to Ben about as they herded the rest of the group into the correct cars. If they were hoping that Luca had kept her up after they'd walked home together the night before, then they were very wrong.

A REUNION IN TUSCANY

Apart from the metaphorical way where they were completely correct.

Because while Luca had slept in his own room, far away from her, Daphne had lain awake until the sun was creeping through her curtains, thinking about what he'd said.

'Daphne, I thought you were my for ever.'

Did he mean it? Or was it just a dramatic, romantic... Italian thing to say? Was he trying to make her feel guilty? Or had it even been a joke? Was he poking fun at the drama of young love? Or...

Or had she really broken his heart when she'd left Tuscany fifteen years before?

And what about what happened next? For a long moment there, she'd honestly believed he was about to kiss her. Her breathing had turned shallow, her skin hot, and she'd licked her lips in anticipation...

And then he'd kissed her forehead and left her alone on the terrace.

What was she supposed to make of that?

Daphne sighed as she settled into her seat. She wanted to know what was going through Luca's head—and she knew the only way to find out was to ask him. But...what if she didn't like the answer?

She needed to figure out what *she* felt about everything before she could ask him about his feelings. Had she wanted him to kiss her? Yes, obviously. Would it have been a good idea? Less certain.

In just a couple of days she'd be leaving again, heading home and back to her boring life. She was never going to be the adventurous, ambitious girl he'd thought she was when they'd first met. If she was honest with herself, she knew that one of the reasons she hadn't told him she was leaving back then was because he might be disappointed in her. Not for going home to look after her mother, he'd understand that, she was sure. But because she'd known even then that if she went back, she wouldn't be leaving again.

Her life would unfold exactly the way everyone had always expected it to—exactly the way that it *had*. No travel, no writing, no adventures.

And she wasn't sure Luca would understand that. She'd seen how surprised he'd looked when they'd talked about her life since they'd parted—one of the reasons she'd tried to push to talk about his more than hers.

She wasn't the girl he'd thought she was. Never had been.

So who had he really wanted to kiss? A girl he thought he knew fifteen years ago who'd never really existed? And what for? Closure, so

114 A REUNION IN TUSCANY

they could walk away on better terms this time? That might be okay—that could be lovely, actually. But she didn't think she could pretend to be anything other than what she really was this time around.

She rested her forehead against the glass of the window. For a holiday, this week was proving surprisingly complicated—and emotional.

At least she'd have a day away from the villa, strolling through the nearest vineyard and tasting the wine, before she had to face him again and try to figure it out.

Except there he was now, climbing into the driver's seat of their four-by-four.

What the hell?

'Everybody strapped in?' Luca certainly didn't sound like he'd lost any sleep over their conversation. He was bright and cheery and looking as hot as ever, damn him. 'I'm afraid Theo just remembered some things he had to do around the villa today, so I'll be your chauffeur to the vineyard in his place—as long as nobody objects.'

Obviously, none of the other guests—all keen cooks and probably rabid Luca Moretti fans—objected. Even Erin shot her a mischievous grin from her seat beside him in the front—chosen because she got car sick. Daphne would not be popular if *she* objected, and the other car—driven by Ben—had already pulled away. Nothing for it but to hunker down and try to sort through her remaining thoughts about last night's conversation without being distracted by Luca's arm resting on the window, or his eyes in the rear-view mirror.

Damn it.

The vineyard was only a half hour drive away, fortunately, and Daphne made sure to throw herself fully into the instructions and tasting portion, keeping her distance from Luca for as long as possible. But once that part of the day was over, and they were told to enjoy the surroundings for a little while before lunch, all her best avoidance tactics failed.

Even Erin darted away when Luca made an immediate beeline for Daphne. 'Some best friend you are,' Daph muttered after her. Erin, standing in the shade with Ben, just grinned in reply.

'Fancy a walk?' Luca offered her his arm.

Daphne stared at it. 'Didn't we do enough of that last night?'

'Last night is kind of what I wanted to talk to you about.'

Literally everyone was watching them. Daphne could feel their gazes boring into her, hotter than the sun. Heaven only knew what they thought had happened between them the night before, but she was sure it was more fun and less unsettling than the truth.

'Maybe somewhere more private?' Luca suggested, dropping his voice so only she could hear. 'Please, Daph.'

Of course she said yes. She'd never been any good about saying no to him—one of the reasons she'd left without telling him that summer. If he'd asked her to stay…she'd have still had to say no, but it would have been a hell of a lot harder.

The vineyard was a sprawling green oasis between sunburnt paths and the browning grass of the nearby hills. Summer here had been scorching, but the green vines and their grapes remained lush and well-watered as they weaved their way between the stakes.

Daphne let Luca take the lead, following him down between the vines and over to an olive grove just beyond, where there was a conveniently placed bench that gave a fantastic view back over the property. He motioned for her to sit and she obeyed, sweeping her skirt out from under her and trying to ignore the hammering of her heart.

'…*you were my for ever.*'

He couldn't still feel that way, could he?

Luca settled beside her on the bench, close enough that she could feel his thigh brush against hers as he jiggled his leg, obviously uncertain about where to start.

'If this is about last night—' Daphne started, but he cut her off.

'It is. And it isn't.' Luca sighed. 'Look, I'd had a little too much wine—a result of spending time listening to my family mock my youth, no doubt—and the moon was out and it all felt…like it happened yesterday. And I might have got a little carried away.'

'*…my for ever.*'

He didn't mean it. Of course he didn't mean it.

'Right, yes.' Daphne swallowed and looked away. 'Of course. Don't worry about it.'

Luca caught her hand where it sat in her lap and pulled it over to rest on his leg, and she turned to look at him as he'd obviously intended. His gaze was steady and serious, unaffected by the surroundings or the wine now.

'I don't want there to be any misunderstanding here, Daph,' he said quietly. 'I *was* heartbroken when you left. I really did hope you'd stay. And yes, I was probably a miserable idiot for my family to mock for a while afterwards.'

The tension was back in her stomach again. She could almost hear the *but* coming.

'But I realise now…you were right. Everything you said last night. I had big dreams and if you'd stayed, if we'd stayed together, the odds are that I never would have achieved them.' His lips jumped up into an ironic sort of half smile. 'You leaving me felt like the worst thing in the world when it happened. But it's also the reason I have a life I love, and that I had the courage to go after my dreams and make them happen. So really, I should be thanking you.'

'For breaking your heart?' It seemed unlikely.

Luca's expression turned utterly serious. 'One thing I have learned over the last fifteen years is that love and ambition don't mix. I wanted an incredible, extraordinary life, and I worked hard to get it. But there's not a lot of time or attention or energy left for romance in that life.'

'Isn't that lonely?' Daphne asked without thinking. Because she knew *she* found it lonely. She hadn't gone after her own version of a big, ambitious life—she'd done exactly what was expected of her. And still, some days she felt so lonely she could cry.

If it wasn't for Erin and Olly, she wasn't sure what she'd do.

'Lonely?' Luca echoed, as if the idea had never even occurred to him. 'I guess it can be. But honestly, I'm usually too busy—or too exhausted—to notice.'

'That's kind of sad,' she said honestly.

'Perhaps.' Luca shrugged. 'I got what I wanted. And I didn't want… I didn't want you to feel bad about it.'

But she *did* feel bad. Not for leaving Luca that summer—she knew it had been the only decision she could make. But because he'd gone out there and turned that heartbreak into an incredible dream life, exactly as he'd always talked about.

Whereas she'd left all the dreams she'd had that summer behind in Tuscany, where they'd withered and died. She'd headed right back into the life she'd always expected to have rather than reach out and try for anything new.

She'd had reasons for that. Good ones. But—

Oh, God. She'd never explained to him why she'd had to leave. She honestly hadn't thought it would matter that much to him at the time. But it had, clearly, and…

Well, maybe it was never too late to come clean.

Luca knew the instant the mood changed—he just didn't know what had changed it. He'd tried to be honest and open, to take away any of the guilt he'd caused her in their late-night conversation, before he moved onto the more interesting part—getting to know the woman he was here with now. But when Daphne shifted on the bench, her leg pulling away from his, and looked up to meet his gaze…he knew that she had more to say—and that whatever came next was about more than just one drunken conversation.

'I… I meant what I said last night,' Daphne said after a moment. 'That I thought you'd be relieved that I'd gone. I really thought that you asking me to stay, to go with you while you hunted your dreams, was a spur-of-the-moment thing, you know? I didn't realise you really meant it.'

Luca shook his head. 'It was wrong of me to ask, anyway. I mean, I was asking you to put your whole life on hold at twenty-one to follow me around while I chased *my* dreams? You said you wanted to travel the world and I was trying to keep you in Italy. Who the hell did I think I was?'

Daphne gave him a faint smile. 'Perhaps. But the thing is…because I thought I was just a summer fling to you I didn't think you'd care about the real reason I had to leave. Or maybe I just didn't want to end things on such a downer. It had been such a glorious summer and… I guess I just wanted to remember it the way it was, rather than letting the real world in to ruin it.'

'The real world?' Luca blinked twice at her,

trying to process her words. 'Wait. You *had* to leave? Why?'

She sighed. 'Because my father called. My mother…she'd been taken sick, had to go to hospital, and my dad was losing it, trying to take care of her and my siblings *and* the business, so I had to go back. He needed me.'

'There was no one else who could help?' Luca took her hand in hers, almost unconsciously. 'You were twenty-one. Why was it all your responsibility?'

'Because I loved them,' she said simply. 'And they needed me.'

'Was your mother okay?' He didn't know what else to ask.

Her smile was brittle. 'That time, yes. She came home, anyway. She…she never fully recovered, though. And she died a few years later.'

'Leaving you to take over all the responsibility for the family, I'm guessing.' That was why she'd never followed her own dreams. Finally, something was starting to make sense.

She looked away, but didn't answer.

'I'm sorry,' he said. 'For your loss. For everything.'

Maybe he'd been fortunate—hell, he *knew* he'd been fortunate. He'd never had that kind of responsibility on his shoulders, and he avoided it even now. He was responsible for the people who worked in his restaurants and his business, but that was all. And most of them were anonymous faces, so while he did all he could to do his best by them, it wasn't the same as family.

Even with his *actual* family he was able to swan in and out as it suited him, while his aunt and uncle took care of Nonna and the restaurant. His father, of course, would never need to rely on anyone else he wasn't paying to perform a service.

Luca was a free agent. And suddenly he realised that Daphne never had been.

Even that summer, the way she'd talked about her family... He hadn't realised what it meant at the time, but in light of this revelation it became much clearer. She'd felt responsible for every one of them, even though she was barely more than a child.

He wondered how long before he'd met her she'd felt that way too.

All those dreams she talked about...she never really believed she could have them.

'I did... I did try to stay,' Daphne said suddenly. 'Or to come back, at least. I needed to go home and see my mum—'

'Of course you did! Daph, I don't blame you for that. If I'd known—'

'No, I know. I just mean...' She took a deep

breath, and this time he waited, let her say what she needed to. 'I'd hoped that, once Mum was better, I might be able to come back. Find you. It was going to be…romantic. I mean, I still thought you probably wouldn't want me here full time, but I missed you and we were so good together… I thought I could at least visit.'

'I'd have liked that,' Luca said softly. She'd had his name, Ben's address at the villa, he was online…she could have found him, if she'd wanted to. He'd left that ball in her court though, too heartbroken and too proud to go searching for someone who didn't want him. 'Why didn't you?'

'Because…the longer I stayed away, the more Italy felt like a dream. Like something too special for someone like me.'

The raw vulnerability in her voice caught in his chest and he pulled her hand closer so she had to turn and look at him.

'Who told you that?' he asked in a whisper. 'Who told you that you don't deserve the whole damn world? *Nothing* anyone could give you, no life you could imagine, could be too special for you. So tell me, who made you believe that?'

'I… I don't know. I guess my dad, maybe?' Luca felt a swell of anger at her admission, and from the way her eyes widened the emotion

124 A REUNION IN TUSCANY

must have shown on his face. 'He didn't mean to! He just… The way he grew up was the way he brought us up. That you were grateful for your lot in life and didn't ask for more. We had a loving family, a successful small business we ran together…until Mum got sick we had literally nothing to complain about. It felt wrong to want more than that, when Dad had worked so hard to give it to us in the first place.'

Luca was trying to understand, he really was. But he'd grown up in a family that had everything money could buy, and he'd still known it wasn't enough, even when he was small. His mother had been unhappy—that was just a fact he'd known all his life. And after she was gone…his father had been shut off completely, and Luca hadn't seen his mother's family again until he was in his twenties, so… He'd always known there was more out there. And he'd wanted it. Believed in it.

Gone after it.

But Daphne hadn't.

'That summer, you talked about so many dreams,' he said, steering them carefully around the rocks in their conversation. She loved her father, he knew, and he wasn't about to argue with her about that. 'You wanted to study more—for your master's degree, right? And you wanted to travel, of course, and write about it. Have you managed to do any of that? Even just holidays? Or evening courses?'

He hated the thought that her whole life had been subsumed by what her family needed from her. But at least he was finally getting to see the real woman she was, the life she'd been hiding from him.

Daphne pulled her hand away from his. 'Not really. My last boyfriend, Henry, didn't really like to travel. And the one before that travelled a lot for work so wanted to stay home the rest of the time. And the one before that never had the money and…well, it just never seemed to happen. I could have gone alone, I suppose. But then Dad needed me at the print shop, too. And my brother and sister had exams and university applications, and life was just…busy.'

'Busy taking care of everyone else's needs,' Luca said. 'What about yours?'

Daphne shrugged, and looked up to meet his gaze at last. 'I guess I always figured there'd be time for those later.'

His breath caught. *Later.* Could later be now? Did he want it to be?

'Daph, I—'

From along the path, he heard Ben calling their names. 'Luca! Daphne! Time to get back to the cars.'

A REUNION IN TUSCANY

With a reluctant smile, Luca got to his feet and held out a hand to pull Daphne to hers.

'This conversation isn't over,' he murmured as they returned to Ben and the others.

He'd pulled away to go say goodbye to their hosts before she replied. But he was almost sure he heard her whisper, 'Good.'

The next day was their last full day in Tuscany, and Daphne was determined not to waste it.

Whether it was the sun, the wine-tasting or the conversation with Luca, she'd returned to the villa the night before with a raging headache and taken to her bed rather than face everyone any longer. It didn't help that she knew they were all whispering behind her back about what the story might be between her and Luca.

'I'd tell you if I knew,' she murmured to herself as she opened her bedroom door to head out that morning.

'Tell me what?' Erin, fresh-faced and wearing a bright pink sundress, stood with one hand raised to knock on the door. 'That you're feeling better, I hope. We have to make the most of our last day!'

'Absolutely,' Daphne agreed with a slightly pained smile.

She couldn't help but feel a little guilty that so far her girls' trip with Erin had involved her

SOPHIE PEMBROKE 127

spending far less time with her best friend than the man she'd known fifteen years ago. On the other hand, after their emotional conversation the day before, Daphne was more sure than ever that finding closure with Luca might be the one thing that helped her move on in her life. Maybe even do some of those things she'd always dreamed of.

Breakfast had been laid out on the terrace for them, with fresh coffee in cafetières at regular intervals, pastries and ripe fruit and yogurts and meats and cheese and everything else they could want. Most of the rest of the group were already sitting around the long table, helping themselves, so Daphne grabbed a plate and followed suit.

While usually the last day of the course featured a celebratory feast, this week they were going one better, according to Ben and Theo. A local couple were getting married at the villa that afternoon and everyone was invited—as long as they also helped with the preparations of the venue and the food.

There was no sign of Ben and Theo, so she assumed they were already busy with wedding prep. There was no sign of Luca either, but she wasn't ready to go looking for him just yet, anyway.

She'd felt like such an idiot after the conversation the day before. In just a few sentences Luca had managed to articulate all the ways that she'd been wasting her life for the past decade and a half, while also reminding her of all the dreams she'd let fall by the wayside.

They'd both talked that summer about walking away from the lives that were expected of them, but he was the only one of them who had actually done it. Instead, she'd let other people tell her what she should do and when for most of her adult life.

She didn't regret going home that summer— her mother had been sick and her family really did need her. And she couldn't regret the last years she'd spent with her before she'd died either.

But what about since then?

Had she really never travelled just because other people—her boyfriends, her father, her siblings—didn't want her to? Because it didn't suit *them*? How many times had Erin invited her away with her and Olly and some of their other friends on trips abroad? And how many times had she said no because her boyfriend didn't fancy it, or her dad said it would be a hassle to get someone to cover for her, or because one of her siblings needed her to drive them somewhere or help out with something?

All of them.

And what about her studying? Of course she could have looked at evening classes. It wasn't that she hadn't thought about it. But it was always inconvenient to someone else, so she'd given up on the idea. Even though *that* was inconvenient to her.

Yes, maybe an evening class wouldn't have been the same as studying full-time for her master's, but it would have been *something*. Something that was hers, that she wanted for herself.

But she hadn't even tried.

And at least some of that had to be on her. If it had mattered enough to her, she'd have found a way around those excuses, wouldn't she?

So why hadn't she?

Who made me believe I don't deserve those things?

She'd been asking herself that question ever since Luca had posed it the day before.

And now, finally, walking out onto the terrace at Villa della Luna, watching the sun snake higher in the sky over the hills and the olive trees, and catching snatches of conversation and laughter in the grove below, she knew the truth.

She had.

She'd convinced herself—with help, sure, but ultimately by herself—that what other people needed and wanted mattered more than she did. That other people's dreams were more important than hers—or her.

God, she'd even done it with Luca, hadn't she? She'd told herself that he didn't really want her to stay in Tuscany with him and taken herself off home without ever explaining why she had to go. She'd never looked him up because she'd assumed he didn't really want her to.

She'd made choices for him, and let everyone else make choices for her.

And she was sick of it.

The others had already finished breakfast now; she'd tuned out their jolly conversations while she ate and thought. Daphne pushed her plate away and moved to the edge of the terrace to see what they were all doing now. Whatever it was, she was sure she was supposed to be joining in. And she would, any moment now.

She just needed to follow this train of thought all the way to the end. For once, she needed to not stop herself thinking—and feeling—when it got too hard, or upsetting. She must not just write off her emotions, her wants and hopes and dreams, as unimportant this time.

She, Daphne, and no one else, needed to decide what she wanted to happen next.

Leaning against the intricate metal railings of the terrace, she stared out at the wedding preparations below—the ribbons being tied to chairs, the lace tablecloths that seemed to have been gathered from every house in the village being laid over the long trestle tables, the lights strung in the trees—and made a decision.

'Daphne! Come help me with this!' Erin called from down below, where she appeared to be being swallowed by a tablecloth. Laughing, Daphne hopped down the steps to join her, holding her sunhat to her head as protection against the already overwhelming force of the summer sunlight.

Together, they spread the cloth across the table, weighting it down at the edges with clever golden clip-on weights. Then they moved on to the next table and repeated it, before turning their attention to the loosely hand-tied floral arrangements that were being strewn over them—dusty reds and golds and oranges with hints of green and cream, a perfect Tuscan palate.

With all of them working together, it took no time at all for the place to take shape. Daphne stood back with her hands on her hips to take it all in, from the lights that would twinkle as the sun set to the flowers that would echo the bride's bouquet, to the layered plates and sparkling glasses and polished cutlery that sat on the tables awaiting the guests.

132　　A REUNION IN TUSCANY

'You can see why people want to get married here, can't you?' Erin said, coming to stand beside her to survey their handiwork.

'Absolutely.'

'The villa isn't the *only* reason I'm marrying Ben,' Theo said, joining them. 'But I have to admit, on the days he's annoying the hell out of me I come out here and I picture this and it's an easy decision not to ditch him.'

Daphne and Erin laughed. As much as he might joke about it, it was easy to see when they were together that Ben and Theo adored each other.

'When's the wedding?' Erin asked.

'End of the summer,' Theo replied. 'We've got at least another three client weddings before then. Speaking of which, I'd better go check on how the food is coming for the big event. I think your fellow students are helping assemble the tasting platters for the starters, if you want to join in?'

'Absolutely! I want to learn to make them for my next dinner party.' Erin grabbed Daphne's arm and tugged her towards the kitchen. But before they could get very far, Theo called her back.

'Daphne? Luca's in the other kitchen working on the desserts, but...did you two have an argument or something yesterday? He seems… out of sorts.'

'We didn't argue,' Daphne assured him. 'We just had one of those conversations that we should have had fifteen years ago.'

'Right,' Theo said, obviously confused.

She patted his arm. 'Don't worry. As soon as the starter platters are done, I'm going to get Erin to help me get ready for this shindig tonight. And then I'll see if I can put Luca back in sorts, so to speak, before I leave tomorrow.'

A broad smile spread across Theo's face. 'Well, I think that sounds like an excellent idea. Off you go!'

With a last grin, Daphne spun away to follow Erin into the kitchen. Her decision was made.

She'd never managed to say a proper goodbye to Luca when she'd left Tuscany fifteen years ago. And she intended to remedy that before she departed again tomorrow. It wouldn't be love, it wouldn't be for ever, but it would be a first step.

Because when she got home? She was going to focus on living the life *she* wanted for a change.

CHAPTER SIX

WEDDINGS AT THE villa were always fun. Luca wasn't usually around for many of them, but he knew from his accountant, and from Ben and Theo, how much they supported the finances of the place. Between the cooking school and the celebrations, they were operating well in the black—and even looking at expanding in the next few years.

It was nice to be there to celebrate with them all—and give himself a dry run for Theo and Ben's wedding later in the summer, too. A wedding always had to be special, but theirs had to be completely perfect. He owed them both too much for it to be anything else.

Besides, supervising the creation of the wedding breakfast—not to mention the desserts and cake—in the kitchens of the villa was a great distraction from the way that Daphne had disappeared the night before after their talk. He'd hoped they'd have a chance to continue their conversation that evening, maybe with a little more wine, moonlight and romance, but the moment they'd returned from the vineyard tour she'd disappeared to her room and hadn't come back out. Erin had taken her some food at dinner time and told them she was suffering from a headache.

One Luca was pretty sure he'd induced.

He hadn't meant for their conversation to get so deep and philosophical—or to sound quite so accusatory about her life choices. But he couldn't just sit by and listen to how she'd put herself second her whole adult life without questioning it just a little.

The cookery school students were helping set up the tables and such for the wedding, and then working on assembling the tasting platters that were serving as starters—large pieces of olive wood laden with cured meats, cheeses, olives, bread, tapenades and dips, and lots of other tasty treats. Luca knew Ben and Theo liked to include them in the things their students made not least because they required little actual culinary ability, and were a very transferable skill. They were forever getting tagged in social media photos by ex-students who'd recreated them for dinner parties at home.

Usually, they were just the starting point for the celebratory dinner at the end of the five-day course, where Ben and Theo—and Luca if he was there—would cook the main course for the students instead of the other way around. Tonight, though, they needed ten times the number of platters to feed all the guests swarming up from the village.

The happy couple were one of Nonna's matches, of course, so Luca was sure his own family would be in attendance. What he really wanted to know though was whether Daphne would also make it.

Theo came into the kitchen late afternoon, when things were starting to get really manic, and clapped him on the shoulder.

'It's going to be a good night, Luca. You know why?'

'Because we've all worked really hard, the villa and staff are great at hosting weddings, and this lovely couple deserve a magical night?' he guessed.

'That too,' Theo allowed. 'But also because I happen to know that Daphne's headache is gone, and she's very much looking forward to seeing you at the wedding tonight.'

Luca froze. 'She told you that?'

'She didn't have to.'

'Right.' Theo was working on vibes again. Admittedly, that was how he and Ben had got together in the first place, but as a fortune-telling device it wasn't the most reliable.

'Besides, I just saw her outside, talking to your *nonna*. Trust me, you want to get out there fast.'

Luca stripped his apron off in record time. 'The guests are starting to arrive?'

Theo nodded. 'In droves. The party has officially started. You get out there. I'll make sure everything goes to plan in here until dinner.'

Luca hesitated. 'Are you sure? You and Ben are the hosts here, I'm just visiting. You're the one who should be out there really.'

'You think anyone out there is more interested in seeing me than the famous Luca Moretti?' Theo rolled his eyes. 'Just get out there, man. Before your *nonna* finds some other hot Italian to marry Daphne off to.'

Luca was halfway to the terrace before he realised he was still wearing his kitchen whites.

He showered in record time, yanked on his tux and headed out just as the sun had started to dip lower in the sky. Sunset itself was still a way off, even this late in the summer, but the afternoon light was glorious, setting the landscape alight with reds and golds.

The bride and groom hadn't arrived yet, but the guests were gathering in large numbers. The actual wedding service had taken place in

A REUNION IN TUSCANY

a chapel down near the village, so Luca imagined the wedding party were still taking photos, while the guests had come up to get a head start on the drinking. That was what usually happened, anyway.

Luca paused on the balcony, not wanting to get drawn into conversation with any other guests before he found Daphne and Nonna. From his vantage point he could look out over the whole gathering—but still couldn't see the one woman he was desperate to find.

He scanned the crowd again, his gaze skipping over expensive dresses and the clinking of glasses until he spotted his aunt and uncle laughing with the people who owned the bar across from their restaurant. And wait! There was Nonna, almost hidden between them, taking the arm of the other couple's young daughter and leading her away—presumably towards a young man who would be perfect for her.

But no Daphne. He flipped his attention back to the other end of the crowd, starting again as he clocked all the faces and bodies, trying to find her, growing more frantic as he looked. What if she'd left already? What if, once again, she'd run off without a proper goodbye?

Could he find her again this time? Would he look? Should he?

He gripped the railing tighter, still looking,

so intent on his search that he almost didn't notice the woman coming to stand beside him until she said, 'Who are we looking for?'

He spun to face her. 'You, of course.'

Daphne smiled, slow and only a tiny bit shy, and he let the rest of the world fall away as he took in the vision of her standing there next to him.

Her green eyes sparkled above soft pink lips and her dark hair was swept up at the back of her head with only a few loose curls hanging down. Her dress was a soft, sea foam green, held up by thin straps over her shoulders and dipping low between her breasts. It was caught at the waist with a thin plaited belt before it swept out into waves of fabric around her waist. He reached the golden sandals on her feet and made his way up again, lingering in some of his favourite spots before returning to her beautiful face.

'You look stunning.'

'You clean up pretty well yourself.' She reached out to run her fingers down the lapel of his tuxedo jacket and he felt a thrill rush through him.

He didn't know what had changed since their conversation yesterday, but something clearly had. And he wasn't about to start questioning his good fortune now.

'Theo told me you were talking to my *nonna*,' he said.

'I was.' She looked out over the crowds to where Nonna was holding the arm of a handsome young man in an iron grip as she introduced him to the young woman she'd taken charge of earlier. 'She told me there was nothing she could do for me that I couldn't already do myself, and set me off into the world to find my own…entertainment for the evening.'

'Nonna doesn't deal in entertainment,' Luca pointed out. 'She only deals in true love.'

'Well, maybe that's why she wasn't interested in me.' Daphne shrugged one slim shoulder and stepped away. 'I'm not looking for love tonight. But I might be looking for something else.'

'Something else?' he echoed. Love wasn't in the cards for him either—it would only interfere with his career—but that something else sounded intriguing…

'Mmm…' Daphne hummed. 'I realised yesterday that we never did get a proper goodbye, did we?' Then she turned and, in just a few steps, she disappeared down the steps of the terrace and back out into the crowd, leaving Luca staring after her.

Then he blinked, shook his head and followed.

He wasn't sure quite what game Daphne was playing this evening. But he knew he wanted to win it.

The wedding breakfast was beautiful.

The villa's students had been seated together at the far end of one of the outmost trestle tables and they were enjoying the fruits of their labours—and the nearby grapevines—with raucous conversation and laughter. Daphne joined in, happily sitting beside Erin, but she kept one eye on the next table at all times.

Which was how she knew that Luca kept watching her, too. He'd basically ignored at least three different women who had come to flirt with him before realising he barely even knew they were there and moving on to their next target. He'd mostly talked with Ben and Theo, but even then she could see Theo elbowing him to get his attention from time to time.

Daphne didn't bother looking away when their gazes met. Didn't hide the fact that she was watching him at all. She wanted him to know.

This time, she was doing their last night together properly.

'You'd been here before, is that right, Daphne?' one of the other students asked,

142 A REUNION IN TUSCANY

drawing her attention back to the table. 'To Villa della Luna, I mean. What was it like?'

'Magical,' Daphne replied. 'Just like it is now, except that it was all ours for the summer.'

'I bet.' The woman who'd asked the question propped her head on her hand, her elbow resting on the table, and smiled at her. 'Tell us more!'

'Yes!' Erin said. 'You *never* talk about what actually happened that summer. Tell us everything!'

And for the first time Daphne realised she didn't want to put that summer away in a box, keep it hidden from her family or the world, a secret only she shared. She wanted to talk about it. So she did.

As she wove tales of that long ago summer— the gelato café, the waterfall where they went skinny-dipping, the picnics in the olive groves and the champagne under the stars—she kept one eye on Luca. She wondered if he knew what stories she was telling. If he was remembering them too.

But there was one story she wouldn't tell— the story of their last night. When Luca had been bouncing so excitedly around the villa, making grand plans for their great escape and not listening when Daphne tried to insert even a modicum of reality. He'd had dreams and they weren't subject to logic or reality.

Which was why, after she'd left to take the call from her father, when she'd realised she had to go home, now, she'd never gone back. She couldn't infect his dreams with her real life.

She'd made her own excuses and disappeared into the night without ever saying goodbye.

But not this time.

The leisurely wedding breakfast meandered its way to its conclusion, and there were toasts and speeches and more wine…and then, as the sun set, the band started up and there was dancing.

Daphne almost regretted the strappy golden sandals Erin had forced her into when they were getting ready together, giggling like they were sixteen again and sneaking out at night. They were too high for dancing, too tight for comfort, but they did make her legs look incredible. And she'd had enough champagne to at least try it, so she took to the dance floor with the others—dancing first with Erin, then one of the elderly students who was staying at the villa with them, then with Theo until—

'Can I cut in?' Suddenly Luca was there, his eyes bright in the flickering lights from the candles and the strings of tiny bulbs wrapped around and between the trees. Theo stepped back amicably, arms wide, and Luca stepped into his place.

His palm landed at her waist as his other hand took hers, and Daphne felt every point of contact between them like a candle flame licking at her skin. The band had switched to a slow song now, and couples were mostly just swaying on the makeshift dance floor under the stars.

Luca pulled her closer and she rested her head against his shoulder, remembering the last time they'd danced like this.

'You were telling stories of our summer at dinner,' he said, his voice a low murmur in her ear. 'I couldn't hear them all, but I picked out enough to recognise them.'

'They wanted to know what the villa was like back then,' Daphne said. 'I told them it was magical.'

Her eyes drifted closed as she snuggled against him. If she kept them shut, she could almost believe it was fifteen years ago, and she was going to get things right this time.

'We danced like this on our last night together,' Luca said. 'Do you remember?'

'I remember everything. I remember wishing that night would go on for ever.'

'But it didn't.' Luca's hand tightened at her hip. 'I went inside for something—more champagne, I think—and when I came back you were gone. Ben said you got a phone call…'

'My dad. Calling about my mum.' In an instant, her perfect night had fallen apart around her.

'Right. I wish I'd known that then. I wish… you'd been able to say goodbye.' The vulnerability in his voice made her heart ache.

Daphne pulled back, just enough to be able to look him in the eye when she said, 'I wish I'd done a lot of things differently in my life. But most of all, right now, I wish we'd had the last night together we deserved.'

'So do I,' Luca whispered.

Part of her was screaming to look away, to smile, politely kiss him on the cheek and leave. Acknowledge the past and move on, back to her old life.

But Daphne wasn't listening to that small, scared part of her any more.

So instead, she reached up in her ridiculous heels, her mouth brushing against Luca's ear as she spoke. 'I'm leaving again tomorrow. Maybe we can make up for that lost night right now. What do you think?'

Luca's first thought was that he'd forgotten how to breathe.

His second that all the blood in his body had headed to a central location, fast.

146 A REUNION IN TUSCANY

He didn't share either of those with Daphne, though.

They'd stopped dancing now, were barely even swaying in the middle of the dance floor, but that was okay because no one was watching them. The best man was leading the groomsmen in some sort of complicated group dance on the other side of the dance floor that reminded Luca of peacocks strutting around to display their feathers. All eyes were on them, not Luca and Daphne.

Which was for the best. The lines of his trousers didn't hide much—especially not the evidence of how Daphne's words had affected him.

'Make up for that lost night…' he repeated hopefully, then swallowed. 'I think we could do that. I think we *should* do that.'

Because maybe that was what was missing: closure. Hadn't he talked about that with Ben when she'd arrived at the villa? God, how was that only four days ago?

He'd never had the chance to say a proper goodbye to Daphne, and that was what had screwed him up for so long. The shock of broken expectations. He'd expected her to stay and travel with him and instead she'd disappeared without a word. He needed the closure of that goodbye.

SOPHIE PEMBROKE

147

And this time, he knew exactly what to expect. He wasn't in mad teenage love with her any more, and he wasn't expecting her to stay. Tomorrow morning she'd get on her plane home without a backward glance and that was *fine*.

Tonight wasn't about getting her to stay. It was about saying a proper goodbye.

And he had so many ideas about exactly how to do that.

'Then let's go,' Daphne whispered, taking his hand.

Together, they slipped through the crowds, weaving between couples and sneaking around the edge of the aftermath of the groomsmen's dance. He thought he saw Ben watching them as they disappeared onto the terrace, but he didn't stop to check. He'd talk to his friend tomorrow. They had the wedding to deal with. And Luca…he had other priorities tonight.

He'd half expected Daphne to lead him to the room she'd been staying in that week, but instead she turned the other way, taking the stairs to the room they'd often shared when he'd stayed there fifteen years earlier. The room he'd claimed as his own for good as soon as he'd bought the villa from Ben's father—even though Ben had tried to convince him to take the master bedroom.

'How did you know I'd still have the same

A REUNION IN TUSCANY

room?' Luca crowded Daphne against the wall outside his door, his arms either side of her head, his lips hovering near hers.

Daphne raised her eyebrows. 'Do you?'

'Yes,' he admitted, dipping to press a quick kiss to her mouth. 'But how did you know?'

Her smile slipped from seductive to sad. 'Because sometimes I think neither of us has really moved on from that summer.'

She was right, he knew. But he didn't want wistful reminiscences tonight. That wasn't the kind of closure he was after.

He wanted to remember how wonderful it had been at its height, the two of them together, before he'd said goodbye to it for good. And he wanted one night with this incredible woman he'd grown to know this week—not the girl he'd suffered his first heartbreak over but the woman she'd become. He wanted to show her it was time to go after her own dreams at last. And what better way was there to kickstart her new life than one perfect night together?

So he swept in and kissed the sad smile away from her lips, reaching behind her to run his hands down her back, over her bottom and then back up again. God, her kiss. He'd forgotten how perfect it felt. How her body fitted against his like it belonged there. Dancing had only been the start.

SOPHIE PEMBROKE

'Come inside?'

'Yes,' she whispered.

They fell through the door together, a tumble of hands and lips and touch and kisses. He didn't want to let her go for a moment, couldn't bear for her to be even inches away from him.

He stripped his jacket from his shoulders with ease as they kissed and her clever fingers came up to loosen his bow tie, then unfasten the buttons of his shirt. It was too slow, but at the same time he delighted in the steady, even pace of his agony—wanting his bare skin against hers but loving the anticipation of the moment.

Still, when it came to her dress, yanking the knot of the sash open and slipping the straps from her slender shoulders was all it took to send it flying to the floor. And he had zero complaints about that.

'God, you're so gorgeous.' He took in the vision of her in the half light from the bedside lamps that were still lit, standing there in nothing but a strapless lace bra and panties, and those incredible gold heels. His blood felt like it might burn out of his veins just looking at her.

But Daphne brought a hand up over her stomach and breasts. 'I'm not twenty-one any more.'

'Neither am I,' Luca pointed out. 'But trust me, Daph. I think you're even better.'

A REUNION IN TUSCANY

It was true. Not just physically—although the way she'd filled out into her curves drove him insane. Personally, too. Fifteen years ago, she'd been a girl taking the summer off from reality, running back when it called, and for all they'd talked about hopes and dreams, he realised now that for her it had all been make-believe.

This summer, this Daphne, had the hard conversations. Confronted her past, examined her life and made decisions based on what she found there. This Daphne was looking for closure, just like him.

He'd loved the twenty-one-year-old girl he'd met that summer, but his family had been right—it was a puppyish, immature love.

This woman? Standing in front of him in spiky gold heels and lace, her eyes wide and her hair tumbling out of its clip down over her shoulders?

He respected the hell out of this woman. He knew she was going to go back to her real life this time and tear it up, remake it in the way she needed it to be to thrive. He almost wished he'd be there to watch. And he knew that in other circumstances he'd want to get to know her all over again, maybe even fall in love again, for real this time.

But that wasn't in the cards. This time, he

was the one who had to get back to a real life—
one he'd worked damn hard for over the years
and wasn't about to give up on now.

So, as it was, he was just grateful for this
chance to have one night with her before they
closed the book on the chapter of their lives
they'd shared for good.

He moved in closer again, done looking. He
needed to touch.

'You are incredible.' He pressed a kiss just
under her earlobe, to a spot that always used to
make her squirm—and still did, he noted with
pleasure. 'You're beautiful.' Another kiss, a little lower on her neck. 'Sexy as all hell.' A kiss
to her collarbone. 'And I can't wait to unwrap
the rest of you.'

This time, his kiss hit the curve of her breast,
even as he reached around to unfasten the clasp
of her strapless bra, tossing it aside and reveal-
ing her perfect breasts to him at last. He dipped
lower, wrapping his lips around first one nip-
ple, then the other, revelling in the feel of her
under his lips—and the way her hands were
clenched in his hair as he worked his mouth
over her body.

'I want to taste every inch of you,' he told
her, backing her towards the bed.

Her thighs bumped against the mattress and
she dropped to sit on it, looking slightly dazed.

152 A REUNION IN TUSCANY

Good. He loved that he could still make her look that way.

He ran a hand down her calf. 'Shoes on or off?' They were sexy as hell but they also looked uncomfortable and he really wanted her to be comfortable tonight.

She swallowed, her eyes dark as she looked down at him on his knees between her thighs. 'Off, please.'

He unfastened them one by one and moved them out of the way.

'You realise you're still mostly dressed,' Daphne said.

Luca looked down and realised it was true—his shirt still hung from his shoulders and his bottom half was still fully clothed, even though his desire was putting some strain on his trousers.

'We'll get to me in a minute,' he promised her. 'First, you.'

Reaching up her thighs, never losing contact with her skin for a moment, he pulled down the scrap of lace she was calling underwear and eased it down her legs and over her feet until she was fully bare before him. Never breaking eye contact, she raised one hand and released the clip holding her hair back, sending it cascading fully over her shoulders, not quite long enough to cover her breasts, thankfully.

Luca smiled, pushed her knees further apart, and kissed his way up her skin until he reached the most sensitive parts between her legs and she fell back onto the bed with a moan.

Oh, yes. If this was goodbye, he was definitely going to take his time about it.

'Let's see how many times I can make you scream before I fill you, shall we?' he said with a grin.

And then he set to work.

The answer to Luca's question—how many times he could make her scream before he finally took pity on her and made love to her—turned out to be lots. Daphne had honestly lost count by the time he slid inside her and she finally, finally felt full again.

More than that, she felt like she'd come home.

The way he knew her body still, after all these years. How he stopped to kiss every sensitive point on her skin he'd discovered that summer, then did it again when she reacted well because it seemed to please him to please her.

She'd forgotten that—how much pleasure he seemed to find in *her* pleasure. Or maybe she'd pushed the memory aside, when no one else since had ever lived up to that ideal. It felt wrong to be remembering an ex-lover in bed with a new one, so she'd tried to forget all the ways Luca had made her feel at home in her own body.

But oh, she was remembering now. And she certainly wasn't thinking about anyone but Luca as he moved above her, inside her, his breath hot in her ear, his mouth against her shoulder, his teeth nipping her now and then to bring her back into the moment more fully...

She hadn't believed it could really feel like this. Not any more, and not again. She'd thought this sort of lovemaking belonged to the young and the careless and the free. She'd never imagined she could have the same kind of uninhibited, wonderful sex at thirty-six that she'd had at twenty-one.

But if anything, it was even better. He remembered her body, yes, but he'd obviously learned some new tricks in the intervening decade and a half, too. Because now when he touched her, when he moved, he took her nerve-endings to extreme heights she was sure they'd never scaled together before.

Now, he tilted her hips just a little, her body soft in his firm hands, changing the angle of his thrust until he hit one that made her eyes fly open wide and her mouth form an O shape she couldn't even force sound out of any more.

And then, then…he smirked, and did it again. And again.

Four thrusts and her body started shaking, her every muscle tensing, building towards something…

Her orgasm washed over her in wave after wave, muscles clenching and pleasure swooping through her, the release and relief everything she'd needed for so long already.

Still moving above her, Luca swore and sank in even deeper, his own release quickly following hers.

And then it was just them, panting in the dark, their breath heavy and their eyes bright.

'Stay with me tonight? Until you have to leave in the morning?' he asked in a whisper, their bodies still connected and their hearts still beating double time together.

She should leave. She still needed to pack. Her phone with her alarm was back in her room. But how could she say no to him now?

'Yes,' she murmured, and let herself love the feel of his arms around her for just a little longer.

After all, she'd be leaving in the morning.

CHAPTER SEVEN

LUCA WOKE UP to the sun streaming through the thin gauze curtains, the sound of tyres on gravel through the open windows, and Daphne Brown in his arms for the first time in fifteen years.

He let himself marvel at the moment for a while before moving, reliving the highlights of the previous night in his mind while she slumbered beside him.

Really, he'd assumed his imagination must have exaggerated how good the sex was between them over the years—nostalgia inflating the memory to almost mythical proportions. It turned out, if anything, his memory had been underselling it.

Luca had slept with enough women over the intervening years—and a few before too—to know that it wasn't always like this. No, that it was *never* like this. He'd never felt so in tune with another person, been with someone who moved with him as if she was an extension of his own body, or as if their minds and their nerve-endings were psychically linked somehow. Every single touch or kiss or thrust of the hips was perfectly in sync. It was incredible.

And he was about to say goodbye to it again. God, he must be crazy.

But great sex was one thing. Taking it any further was something else entirely—something they hadn't even discussed. They'd agreed, last night was a goodbye. He'd been pushing his luck even asking her to stay with him—and he'd half expected her to say no. As it was, she'd probably have to get moving fast to catch her plane. What time did Ben say the cars were leaving for the airport? He couldn't remember.

Wait.

Tyres on gravel. That was what had woken him up.

Daphne stirred in his arms before he could follow the thought through to its logical conclusion. He pressed a kiss against her shoulder, enjoying the way she hummed at his touch, then turned around so her bare breasts were pressed against his chest again.

Maybe she didn't have to leave just yet…

'What time is it?' she asked, her voice gravelly with sleep.

158   A REUNION IN TUSCANY

'Mmm, not sure. Hang on.' He reached over her for his phone, which he'd clearly neglected to charge the night before, but had at least managed to toss on the bedside table, on silent since he'd had no intention of being interrupted.

The battery was almost dead, but it turned on long enough for him to check the time before tossing it back where it came from. Whoever the messages and missed calls were from could wait.

'Ten-thirty,' he said, snuggling back down beside her.

'Mmm, okay.' She nestled her head against his chest for a moment, before jerking up to stare at him. 'Wait. What?'

Before Luca could tell what was happening, Daphne was out of his arms, out of the bed and across to the window—apparently unaware she was still completely naked as she ripped open the curtains and stared out.

As it happened, though, it didn't matter. There was nobody there to see.

'They've gone,' she said, sounding lost and confused. 'They left without me.'

Luca forced himself into a sitting position. 'For the airport?'

Nodding, Daphne turned round to face him. 'We must have…overslept. I'm going to miss my plane. I— Oh, God! What do I do now?'

SOPHIE PEMBROKE 159

Leaning over the side of the bed, Luca scooped up his shirt and threw it to her. His mind was whirring, thoughts flying at him a mile a minute—and two possible paths opening up before him. He knew which one he wanted to follow but it wasn't entirely up to him.

In fact, it wasn't up to him at all. It had to be Daphne's choice.

'I'm going to give you two options now,' he said, watching forlornly as she buttoned up his shirt over her beautiful body. It was for the best, he knew—he couldn't be distracted right now when there were decisions to be made. But still... 'You choose the one you want and I will make it happen, okay? And there's no bad feelings or judgement whichever you pick. We had our perfect last night, and our closure. This is a whole new chapter now. Okay?'

Daphne nodded slowly, her fingers pausing on the last button. 'What...what are the options?'

'Option one, you run down to your room now, throw your things in a bag, get changed, and meet me out front. I've got a car here and I will get you to the airport in time for your flight, come hell or high water. Option two...' He trailed off. Should he even ask? It hadn't worked out so well for him last time, after all.

But she hadn't jumped at option one yet.

160   A REUNION IN TUSCANY

Maybe she was waiting for him to ask again. *Wanting* him to.

Daphne's tongue darted out to sweep across her lower lip. 'What's option two, Luca?'

'Stay another week in Tuscany with me,' he said. 'We can go to my apartment in Florence, have a few days to get to know each other again for real, and enjoy what we've rediscovered here. No pressure, no promises, no expectations. Just…a holiday. A break from our real lives before I go back to my work and you… well, I hope you set out to chase your own dreams at last.'

He had to force himself to keep breathing evenly while he waited for her answer. But she hadn't run away yet. That was already an improvement on last time he'd asked her to not fly away home. But he could tell from the line between her brows that she was thinking hard, considering what each of them meant.

Finally, she said, 'Chasing after my long-delayed dreams is going to be a lot of work. I need to…process a lot, figure out how to make everything work out, because it's not like I'm going to abandon my family suddenly. It's going to be a long-term project, redefining my life my way. And that takes planning, and thought, and dreaming.'

'It does.' Luca's spirits started to sink. Of

course she wanted to get back to her new dream life straight away.

'So I think, if it's okay with you, I'm going to take option two, and do some of that thinking here in Tuscany, with you. After all, it's where it all started, isn't it? And you've done it before—giving up everything and chasing a new life. Maybe you've got some tips?' Her smile spread across her face, and Luca felt a wolfish grin cover his own in return.

'In that case, you're really not going to need that shirt after all…'

By the time they made it out of bed again, Ben and Theo were back from the airport. With a last kiss at the bedroom door, Daphne left Luca to go speak with his friends, while she showered, changed and packed up her stuff to leave for Florence.

Obviously, she also spent the time having an existential crisis.

'What was I thinking?' she asked her reflection in the mirror as she dragged a wide-toothed comb through her wet hair. 'He was offering to get me to the airport. I could have left!'

But she hadn't. If she was brutally honest with herself, she hadn't even really considered it. Because last night's goodbye had felt so much more like the start of something than the end…

When she picked up her phone she found messages and calls from Erin, starting early that morning and growing steadily more panicked until the one that read:

Okay, we're leaving for the airport now. I didn't want to go without you, but Theo promises they'll make sure you get home safely. And if you're with Luca… I want details when you get back to London!!!

She'd have to call her soon but she'd still be on the plane, so she just sent a quick reassuring message for now. The proper phone call debrief would have to wait. Besides, Erin would want to know what her plan was now, and how it was all going to work, and Daphne definitely didn't have any answers for that yet.

She did, however, have to warn her dad that she wouldn't be back. First, though, she checked in with Scott, who was covering for her at work in the print shop, that he was okay to take control for another week. He sounded so excited Daphne almost felt sorry for him— except that it was exactly what she needed.

She thought about calling home, but instead settled for sending a message to the family

SOPHIE PEMBROKE 163

WhatsApp group, so her dad, brother and sister would all get it at the same time.

Having such a great time in Tuscany I've decided to extend my stay by another week. Scott is fine looking after the shop for me, so I'll see you all when I get back!

Then, as a slightly guilty afterthought:

Hope everything is well with all of you!

Then she turned off her phone before she could find out.

Because she already knew it wouldn't be. Dad would be having a problem with the microwave or the telly that only she could fix, or the supermarket shop she'd arranged to have delivered after he got back from staying with Aunt Sharon would have the wrong sort of carrots in it or something. Caitlin would be having some sort of friend drama she wanted to stress out about with her, and Tommy would have been planning on asking her to do something or other she now wasn't there to do.

But for once, they were all going to have to manage without her.

'There are other people in the world they can depend on to solve their problems,' she

164   A REUNION IN TUSCANY

told herself. Then she stopped. 'Or, actually, they could just try fixing them themselves for a change.'

It wasn't as if Dad couldn't get out to the supermarket. He was happy to go there to buy his beer or his lottery ticket. And Caitlin's friend dramas really weren't anything to do with her. And Tommy…he was an adult, with a job. He could pay for a taxi or a train to wherever he wanted to go that he was hoping she'd take him.

They were all capable of taking care of themselves for a week.

They'd have to be, because Daphne was taking care of *herself,* for the first time in a really long time.

Bags packed and ready, she took one last look at the room she'd been staying in, then shut the door behind her and went to find Luca.

The villa was strangely quiet, after a week of being full of conversation and chatter and cooking with the other students—and especially after the raucous fun of the wedding the day before. Daphne padded down the tiled corridors until she reached the kitchen, Ben and Luca's voices floating out to her long before they came into view.

'Are you sure this is a good idea, man?' Ben said, and Daphne paused instinctively, just out of view.

Eavesdropping was wrong, she knew that. But if they were talking about her…

Luca laughed. 'Are you kidding? Another week of incredible sex with a woman like Daphne? How can it be a *bad* idea?'

'Because it was never just sex between you two,' Ben said. 'Remember, I was there for all your broken-hearted rants after she left the last time. Do you really think it's going to be any easier to say goodbye again this time if you spend another week together?'

Daphne bit her lip. It wasn't as if she hadn't had the same worries herself, ever since she'd agreed to stay.

But Luca just scoffed. 'It's not like that. I told you—last night was just meant to be a proper goodbye, nothing more. So think of this week as…a farewell tour, I guess.'

'I'm just saying, don't let yourself get close unless you both agree it means something more this time,' Ben said.

'It won't,' Luca said firmly. 'I'm not in the market for anything more, you know that. Last time, I was a romantic kid who thought the world could run on sex and champagne and love. I know better now. I have ambitions and responsibilities and a career I love. I'm not going to put any of that at risk by falling for some woman I know I can't have a future with, am I? Trust me, this is just a week of fun for both of us. Daph has her whole life to get back to as well—a life I'm not part of either. We both know what we're getting into here.'

Well, if she hadn't before, she did now. And that was a good thing, she reminded herself. She needed to go into this with her eyes open—otherwise she was putting her heart at risk.

Her heart wasn't in play this week. She was staying because Luca had always made her feel more like herself than she ever had left to her own thoughts and feelings—and she needed that if she wanted to go home and make changes in her life. The sort of changes that would help her move forward into the kind of life *she* wanted, not the one that was convenient for everybody else.

She and Luca would have a week of fun and sex and laughter, a week of dreaming big dreams and talking through what she wanted to happen next in her life, and she'd go home with the kind of energy and sense of self she needed to make those changes.

Nothing more. She had to remember that.

'Well, if you're sure you can handle it,' Ben said, and really, he could have been talking to either of them, Daphne thought.

She took a deep breath, picked up her bag

again and strolled into the kitchen as if she'd only just arrived.

'Ready?' she asked Luca, and he jumped down from where he was sitting on the long wooden table by the arched window, a cocky grin firmly in place.

'Always.' He turned to Ben. 'Good to see you, bud. I'll stop by again before I head back to the States if I can.'

'You'd better.' They exchanged a brief hug, before Ben turned to her. 'So good to see you again, Daphne. Look after yourself.' And then, as he leaned in to hug her too, he added in a whisper, 'Look after him, too. Please.'

'I will,' she promised.

Then Luca took her hand and her bags and they walked out of Villa della Luna one last time—only this time they were together.

She hoped they'd have a better ending, this time around.

'Luca, this place is incredible,' Daphne breathed the moment they walked into the apartment. He smiled, glad she liked it, and glad that she was feeling more comfortable again. She'd been quiet on the drive over, and he'd worried she might be about to change her mind—but if anything could convince her to stay, he reckoned it would be the Florence apartment.

He tossed his keys onto the table inside the front door and dropped their bags beside it. 'Want the full tour?'

She nodded enthusiastically, so he guided her through to the main living space.

'The apartment has been in my family for years,' he explained as they walked. 'My dad bought it when he was courting my mother, apparently—and then transferred the deeds to her as a wedding present. When she died, she left it to me. It's where I come when I need to escape everything—even Ben and Theo and Nonna and Aunt Rosa and Uncle Rocco.'

They all knew about it, of course, but none of them had ever been there. In fact, he didn't think he'd *ever* brought anyone back to the Florence apartment before. It had always been his own secret, private space.

But somehow it felt right to share it with Daphne.

'The building is actually a thirteenth-century manor house type thing,' he explained, gesturing up to the ceiling. 'Hence the chandeliers.'

'And the location.' Daphne had moved to the window and was looking out over one of Florence's most famous piazzas. 'I can't believe you can actually *live* here.'

'Yeah, it's pretty spectacular.' He moved behind her, bracketing her hips with his hands

SOPHIE PEMBROKE

as they watched the city go by below. Tourists flocked to the piazza and the famous sights, giving the place a buzz he never grew tired of. 'Did you visit Florence when you were in Tuscany before?' He knew he'd never taken her, but despite his best efforts she'd not spent all of her time in the country with him.

But she shook her head. 'I had hoped to, but somehow it never seemed to happen.' She tilted her head up to look at him. 'Story of my life, apparently.'

His hands tightened on her hips. 'But maybe not any more?' Because she'd chosen to stay in Tuscany with him, despite everything she'd told him about the demands of her family and her life back home.

Maybe she really was ready to make a change this time. And if she was, he intended to help her do it in any way that he could.

'That's the idea,' she said with a smile, and he bent to kiss her lips.

'Right, back to the tour!' Otherwise, he was going to get carried away before they'd even started.

The apartment wasn't large but it didn't need to be, just for him—or for the two of them now. Most importantly, it was so centrally located that almost everything he wanted to show her in Florence—and certainly everything the

A REUNION IN TUSCANY

guidebooks recommended—was within a walk of ten or fifteen minutes or so.

Still, he took the time to show her around the living room, with its mix of antique and modern furniture, and the insanely comfortable sofa he loved to lounge on, and the small bistro table and chairs by the narrow balcony that looked out over the piazza below. Then the kitchen—small but equipped with everything he'd need to whip up almost any meal she fancied. The bathroom, with its marble surfaces and rainforest shower.

'And here are the bedrooms.' He opened both doors one after another, so she could see the master—with its huge iron bed and layers of white linen, the chandelier hanging from the high ceiling above—as well as the second bedroom, with a smaller double bed and more sedate lighting.

Daphne raised an eyebrow at him. 'Do you think we'll be needing both?'

Luca shut the door to the second bedroom with relief.

But the exchange made him realise something. In the heat of the moment, making his offer for her to stay, they hadn't really had a chance to discuss what it meant—besides no pressure and probably sex. His conversation with Ben that morning weighed heavily on his mind.

He was certain about what he wanted out of this trip. But had he been clear enough with Daphne? Boundaries were important. Especially since she had a history of not being able to set them with people she cared about, it seemed to him.

Things were different this time around. Fifteen years ago, he'd have done anything to make her stay, to believe that he loved her, wanted to spend for ever with her—even if, at twenty-one, he wasn't sure he'd even known what for ever looked like.

This time, she'd been the one to make the move last night, to suggest the idea of a last chance to say goodbye. But he'd asked her to stay again, just like fifteen years ago—except this time she'd said yes.

And this time he couldn't give her any more than he'd told Ben he was offering. But he didn't know for sure what *she* wanted. And if he intended to help her start living her life for herself, that mattered.

That was why he'd given her the option of the second bedroom. He wasn't going to assume that she wanted to be in his bed every night they were here until she told him that was what she wanted. Although he had to admit to being pleased that she had.

172   A REUNION IN TUSCANY

So, sleeping arrangements were sorted. Next up: everything else.

'Was there anything in particular you wanted to see or experience in Florence first?' he asked. 'Or would you rather take a walk and see what we see? Or even stay here and relax for a while?'

Options. He had to keep giving her options—at least, in the areas he could offer them. She had to get used to making her own choices, to thinking about what *she* wanted, not what suited him or anyone else.

Daphne tilted her head as she considered. 'Maybe let's just go for a walk today, get a feel for the place. Then we can start the serious sightseeing tomorrow.'

He should have known she'd have plans to see everything. 'Works for me. Let's go, then.'

And once she'd relaxed and settled into this plan he could make sure she understood that he couldn't offer anything more than this week—all while also persuading her to take charge of her own life for a change and stop doing what other people wanted.

Easy, right?

Luca grabbed his sunglasses and keys from the table by the door and wondered, not for the first time when it came to this woman, whether he might have got himself in over his head.

CHAPTER EIGHT

FLORENCE WAS EVERY bit as beautiful as Daphne had always dreamed it would be.

The wide cobblestone streets, the busy piazzas, the incredible buildings, the *museums*—every inch of the place was incredible. They'd spent their first day just wandering, taking in the vibes and the sunshine—although Daphne had been able to tell Luca had been preoccupied by something. Guessing it was probably to do with his conversation with Ben back at the villa that morning, she'd decided to tackle it head on.

When they'd stopped for dinner at a small trattoria where Luca had kept his head down and managed to go unrecognised by the staff and patrons, Daphne had raised the subject.

'There was something I wanted to talk about before we go any further here,' she'd said, and across the table, Luca had frozen. 'I know I've already hinted at it but this time I think we need

174 A REUNION IN TUSCANY

to be really clear. Not talking about things like this is what caused us to spend fifteen years thinking the wrong things about each other, right? So…this week… I'm looking forward to having the time here with you and making the most of it, but that's all it is for me, okay? A holiday fling. When it's over, it's over. I'm going back to the UK to find the life *I* want to lead for a change, and I don't need any…entanglements complicating that for me. It's going to be difficult enough as it is. But at the same time… I don't want it to be awkward.'

Luca's shoulders had visibly relaxed at her words, and she'd known she'd done the right thing. Every word of it was true, too.

She had bigger plans for her life now than regressing to the twenty-one-year-old romantic she'd once been.

The only problem with that declaration was that, with their extra week ticking away by the day, it was getting harder to imagine what else in the world she might want her life to be. Because exploring the cathedrals and cafés of Florence with a handsome celebrity chef by day and exploring each other's body by night? That was pretty much the dream right now.

Maybe it was just the city. Florence really was more incredible than she'd ever thought it could be, and Luca was an excellent guide.

He'd obviously spent a lot of time there over the years, and he introduced her to parts of the city she was sure weren't in the usual guidebooks. Even restaurants and bars where he knew the staff by name—and spoke to them in fluent, flowing Italian that made her blood heat up every time. She was getting the personalised Florentine experience, and she loved it.

She couldn't believe she'd been so close to Florence fifteen years ago and never visited, simply because it might have been inconvenient for someone else.

Now, as she sat sipping black coffee at an outdoor café table on the edge of the piazza below Luca's incredible apartment, she considered for a moment how her life might have been different if she *had* visited the city back when she was twenty-one. Would she have been inspired to have her own renaissance? Maybe.

Perhaps if she'd visited Florence with Luca then, she'd have found it impossible to leave at all. Or at least, if she'd visited it alone, she might have made plans to come back sooner or visit other places on her bucket list.

But she hadn't. It was all very well imagining the lives she might have led, but she was living this one. And with only two days left in Florence, she still didn't know what she wanted her life to look like when she left.

A REUNION IN TUSCANY

Part of the reason for that, she'd decided, was that it was just so damn hard to think about anything except the present when she was with Luca. Whether they were touring a cathedral—and he was whispering interesting facts about it in her ear—or they were eating gelato—and he was licking it from her fingers—or they were out for dinner—and they were talking about anything and everything for hours until the waiters had to ask them to leave so they could close—when they were together, he was all she could think about. And it only got worse when they returned to the apartment together at night. When he kissed her, touched her, made love to her...her brain simply ceased to function.

It was actually pretty glorious.

But also not conducive to planning her life. So when Luca had apologetically told her he had to take a work call that morning, she'd told him not to worry and skipped down the steps to the piazza for a coffee and some serious deep thought.

She had two more days in Florence with Luca, and then she was back to the real world. So, what did she want that to look like?

Daphne pulled the new notebook she'd bought for her trip from her bag and flipped through the first few pages, where she'd scribbled down some of her thoughts and impressions of the places she'd visited since she'd arrived in Italy. They were rough, of course, but she could still feel herself falling into the memories as she reread.

She loved this. Loved writing about the places she'd been. She wanted to do more of it—maybe as a career, but at least as a hobby. That couldn't be too hard a place to start, could it?

She turned to the next blank page and started to jot down ideas.

Travel more—take solo holidays?
Start a travel blog—record my travels, practice my writing...build an audience?
Maybe take a night class? Creative writing? Or a language? Might help with the travelling?
Talk to Dad about the shop.

That last one took her a while to even admit to herself. The family business her father was so proud of was doing well enough, but running it was simply soul-destroying for her. Scott seemed to love it, in a way she never had. Maybe it was time to start handing off more of the responsibility for it to him and start figuring out how she could build the sort of career she wanted instead. Was freelance travel writer a thing? She could find out. Maybe even write a book... If Scott took over the shop, she'd have the time to travel *and* write about it.

Except Scott wasn't family, and her father would never accept someone who wasn't a Brown by blood or marriage running things.

And she definitely wasn't coercing Scott into marriage, just so she could find a new job.

Marriage. Well, that just started a whole new train of thought for life ambitions, didn't it?

Did she want to get married? Daphne tapped her pen against the page and considered the question.

Yes, some day. If she found the right person.

The men she'd been dating so far were all wrong for the new life she was picturing. The one thing they all had in common was that they needed her to boost their egos and facilitate them going after *their* dreams, while she ignored her own. She definitely wasn't doing that any more.

So what was she looking for instead?

Glancing over her shoulder to make sure that no one was watching, she started a new list on the next page, feeling a little like a hormonal teenager as she titled it 'My Perfect Man'.

She didn't bother with notes about looks—that wasn't the part that worried her. Attraction was one thing, and honestly, she was pretty confident in her ability to judge in the moment whether she had chemistry with someone—especially now she'd had a reminder from Luca on what that felt like.

No, the part that tripped her up was seeing what a guy was really like, under the nice words and the dinners and the kisses. The part that told her who he really was.

Who did she want him to be, this mythical man she might marry?

He needs to be kind, to me and to others.

She'd had too many dates with men who fawned over her only to be rude to the waiter to put up with that kind of behaviour. She wanted someone who treated the kid washing the dishes with the same respect as the owner, the way Luca had at the restaurant he'd taken her to the night before, where he'd been friends with the head chef and they'd got a tour of the kitchens.

He needs to be interesting, and self-aware, and take responsibility for his own life, the way I am with mine now.

She wasn't looking for someone who could

only talk about themselves, their work, or all the things that were wrong in their life. When she'd met her last ex, Henry, he'd seemed like a kind, funny and interesting person. But in no time, all their conversations seemed to be about the unfairness of being made redundant, or all the reasons his marriage breakdown was his ex-wife's fault.

Luca was a great example of all those things. Even after he'd told her how badly she'd broken his heart, he'd come back the next day to explain how, actually, if she hadn't, his life wouldn't have turned out the way it had, so in a way he was grateful.

And even though he'd had so many financial advantages growing up, he'd been conscious of his privilege—and turned his back on it all to make his own success. He never really complained about how his father's behaviour after his mother's death had impacted him, he'd just found a way around it. She admired that.

What else?

He has to have his own dreams, but it would be perfect if some of them were the same as mine, like travelling and learning.

Exploring Florence with Luca had been so much fun, and she wanted more of that in her life. Even when they were visiting places that he'd been before, he was still keen to learn new things about them.

So, where did that leave her?

She read through her list again and bit her lip as she realised the truth.

The relationship she was looking for…

It was the one she was already having with Luca.

The one she'd be walking away from in two days' time. The one they'd both agreed couldn't last exactly *because* of that last point. She needed to chase her dreams and he'd already found his. He had a career he loved and a responsibility to his employees. He wasn't going to give that up—and she would never ask him to.

Which meant this ended at the end of the week, however perfect it felt.

Swallowing hard, Daphne tore the page out of her notebook, folded it up and shoved it into the dregs of her water glass, watching her list melt away as the ink hit water.

She was going after her dreams, yes. But some dreams were just too impossible to admit to.

Even to herself.

Luca was starting to think he should have just driven Daphne to the airport that morning after the wedding after all. Not because he wasn't enjoying her company in Florence—quite the opposite. Because the longer he spent with her, the harder it was getting to imagine saying goodbye.

Damn it. Ben was right.

He hated it when Ben was right. He'd be all smug about it later, if Luca ever admitted it to him. Which he wouldn't.

He'd managed to put off almost everything work-related since his last call with his manager, but that morning's meeting really couldn't be postponed. Which was unfortunate since, after waking tangled up in the sheets with Daphne and making long, leisurely love to her, before she walked naked to the bathroom with a swing in her hips for a shower, work was the last thing he was interested in.

He was spending a morning he could have spent in bed with Daphne talking about profit and loss statements and marketing plans instead. The world just didn't seem fair.

Finally, the damn thing was done and he ended the call, grabbed his phone and his keys and raced for the door to find Daphne... and then stopped. Because reality had finally caught up with him.

I have ambitions and responsibilities and a career I love. I'm not going to put any of that at risk by falling for some woman I know I can't have a future with, am I?

He remembered saying those exact words to Ben, just a few days earlier in the kitchens at Villa della Luna. And yet here he was, rushing through a meeting he *knew* he hadn't given his full attention simply because he hadn't kissed Daphne in an hour or two.

'What am I doing?' he whispered to himself, then banged his head lightly against the still shut front door. 'Hell, *what* am I doing?'

It wasn't a rhetorical question. He knew the answer, he just didn't want to admit it. Because if he admitted it, he'd have to do something about it.

He had two more days in Florence with Daphne. Couldn't he just plead ignorance a little longer?

But it was no good. Reality had come knocking and he couldn't ignore it any longer.

He'd fallen in love with Daphne Brown. Again.

And if he didn't walk away soon, he might never be able to. Not without shredding his heart into more pieces than she had last time.

He'd *promised* himself he wouldn't do this. That his career, his dreams, his future mattered more than any woman. And he'd believed

184 A REUNION IN TUSCANY

it, too. But here he was all the same, another damn fool for love.

Oh, this was going to end badly, whatever he did. Because it wasn't just his future at risk here.

Daphne had her own life to go back to, one she was finally going to start living on her own terms. He'd promised himself that he'd help her achieve that, this time. The last thing she needed was him hanging around, dragging her down—or worse, dragging her along with him to chase his own ambitions. She'd spent too long pandering to other people's dreams and he wouldn't ask her to do that a moment longer, especially not for him.

So even if she felt the same, even if she wanted something more with him, it wouldn't be fair to put her in that position by asking, not when she was so close to figuring out things for herself.

He'd watched her this week, getting more confident in her own decisions and opinions. He'd tried to leave their activities open to her to decide—after all, he could explore Florence any time he wanted. When she'd asked for opinions or information he'd given them, but the decisions had all been hers.

And it wasn't just on the tourist trail that he'd let her take the lead. While he enjoyed taking control in the bedroom, he wasn't one of those men who *always* had to be in charge. It had been fun and liberating for both of them to take turns with that, each exploring new ideas and feelings together. He got the impression that Daphne hadn't had much of a chance to chase her own pleasure over the past fifteen years, and he had loved every moment of her figuring out what she wanted and needed from her body and his—and helping wherever he could.

It had been perfect, these past few days in Florence. And that was the whole problem.

Perfect couldn't last.

It wasn't fair to weigh her down with his feelings. But he couldn't torment himself much longer either.

Their last night at the villa was supposed to have been goodbye, and now they were just dragging it out. Thinking about *actually* saying goodbye to this happy bubble they'd created together made his chest ache. Maybe he should call time on it before it got any more painful.

Besides, even if he *did* ask her to extend her stay again…the chances were, she'd say no. Or if she agreed that it wouldn't last. Sooner or later, she'd leave him again, just like she had fifteen years before—either at the first distress call from her family, or because she realised she couldn't have the life she wanted with him in tow. Only this time, he wasn't sure if he could survive the heartbreak.

No, there were just too many reasons this wouldn't work. Which meant he needed to end it before he fell any further.

His head back in gear, Luca made his way much more slowly down the stairs from the apartment to the piazza. It took no time for him to find Daphne, sitting outside one of the little cafés that lined the square. She appeared to be frowning at a piece of paper that had been dunked in her water glass, and so didn't spot him until he was almost at the table.

'Everything okay?' he asked, curious as to what had been on that paper. Whatever it was, it was gone now.

She nodded and pushed the glass aside. 'And you? How was the meeting?'

'Boring.' He held a hand out to pull her up. 'Come on. We're missing out on important sightseeing time.'

Because if he was going to end this little adventure early, he needed to make the most of the brief time they had left together. After that...

Well. He'd made it fifteen years without seeing her before.

He was sure he could make it the rest of his life after this.

Couldn't he?

* * *

Something had changed, and Daphne wasn't entirely sure if it was her fault or Luca's. Or maybe they'd both reached the same conclusion independently. Or, worse, different conclusions. She'd never know unless she was brave enough to ask.

And taking charge of her own life that way was still a work in progress. She might need a little more time and perhaps a glass of wine or two to work up that much courage.

The point was, there was a distance between them that hadn't been there since they'd arrived in Florence.

Like we're already preparing to say goodbye.

They'd planned to walk up to the Piazzale Michelangelo that afternoon, in time to watch the sun set over Florence, and so, after a leisurely lunch in which they both seemed to be shying away from any sort of difficult or meaningful conversation, they set off up the hill.

It was a bit of a walk, especially in the late summer heat, but Daphne relished it. She needed the physical distraction from everything that was going on inside her head. And if they were a little out of breath, that just made it more understandable that they weren't talking much.

A REUNION IN TUSCANY

The Piazzale Michelangelo had the most fantastic views over the whole of Florence, and Daphne had been looking forward to enjoying them since they'd arrived in the city. She didn't want to be distracted or unsettled. She wanted to focus on the moment.

So that was what she did.

She took in the replica of Michelangelo's *David* with all the other tourists, snapping photos on her phone and even asking some passing Americans to take one of her and Luca together—which was nice, until they recognised Luca and she had to pause her explorations while he signed autographs for a while.

But then they spent time taking in the views, pointing out all the places they'd visited already that week. Luca came to stand behind her, running his hands up and down her bare arms until she shivered from his touch, his voice low and warm in her ear.

At least they still had this. Whatever overthinking was derailing the easy relationship they'd enjoyed so far, the physical connection between them wasn't affected at all. That was something.

The heady heat of the early evening seemed to seep into her bones as they watched the sun start to sink, bathing everything in a golden light.

'It really is magical here, isn't it?' Daphne leaned back into him, his heartbeat a steady thump at her back.

'I've always thought so.' She felt the words in his chest. 'Florence is where I come back to when I need to feel…myself. I guess that's why I hoped it might do the same for you.'

She started a little at that, as certain comments and observations from the last few days started to click into place in her head, making a kind of sense she hadn't even considered before.

'That's why you asked me to stay in Tuscany,' she realised. 'You knew I needed the time to figure out what's next for me. What my life is going to be after this.' She'd told him that was her reason to stay—she just hadn't realised that he'd known it before she did. That everything he'd done since they'd reconnected had been him guiding her to that end.

She'd thought she was doing it for herself, but he'd been steering her in that direction the whole time.

She felt the truth of it in her bones before she felt his slight nod behind her. All those conversations about her life since they'd parted, the dreams she hadn't chased. Every time he'd left the decisions in her hands this week. He'd been trying to guide her back to the girl he'd once known—and the life she'd wanted. Or at least a more grown-up version of it.

She couldn't be cross about it, could she? Not when she'd been planning the exact same thing for herself this week. And yet still it rankled, just a little. That he didn't think she could do that for herself, without him nudging her in the right direction.

Although she hadn't, had she? So maybe he'd been right.

She *wouldn't* be cross, she decided. Not about that. Although…

'Was this just a pity trip?' she asked. She needed to know that much, at least. Because for her it had been so much more. 'Did you ask me here because you felt sorry for me, going back to my boring, predictable life, while you went off to conquer the world?'

Luca's arms tightened around her waist. 'No. Of course not. I asked you to stay because…' He sighed. 'Honestly? I just wasn't ready to let you go yet. That was all. Giving you a bit more time to think about what you wanted from life was a bonus. One you jumped at, by the way.'

'I see.' She believed him. The way they were together…she hadn't been able to give that up either. Even when she knew she should.

She still wasn't sure how she was going to, now.

Although…maybe she didn't have to. Yes,

Luca had been clear about what he could and couldn't offer, but so had she. She'd been firm that this was just one week and then it was goodbye, that she couldn't and wouldn't take anything between them any further.

But if she was changing her mind about that, wishing for more now their time together was coming to an end, didn't it make sense that he might be, too?

She thought he might be. They hadn't talked about love or anything, except in terms of how his much younger self had *thought* he felt about her fifteen years ago. But there were degrees between holiday fling and true love, weren't there? Maybe this could be somewhere between them.

Maybe it could keep growing.

Maybe he *could* love her again, one day, if she gave him the chance.

Because she was already very afraid that she was falling in love with him.

Yes, there were a hundred reasons this couldn't work. Their dreams lay in different places. Fifteen years ago, he'd wanted her to travel with him, but now she'd just be following him around, supporting his career—and that wasn't what she wanted. But he couldn't give up his dreams to chase hers either. That wouldn't work for either of them. It would drive them apart in the end.

But…she'd promised herself that she'd trust her instincts from now on. And her instincts told her that Luca wasn't any more ready to give this up again than she was.

Could it be that they just needed to talk about it, and find a way forward, together? Was that even possible? She couldn't see how.

But her instincts were still screaming at her to try.

And wasn't that the thing about dreams? They always seemed impossible until you found a way to make them happen. She'd *promised* herself she wouldn't live a half-life any more, denying what she wanted.

And she wanted Luca.

Luca kissed the side of her neck, just below her ear, and she felt her whole body react.

'As beautiful as this sunset is,' he murmured, 'nothing is quite as beautiful as you spread out on our bed. Time to go home?'

Daphne nodded, already turning to head back to the apartment.

One more night. One more night and then she'd ask him.

Ask if maybe they could be more than they'd ever managed to be before.

Maybe they could even be for ever this time.

CHAPTER NINE

LUCA WOKE THE next morning to Daphne's lips against his chest, and his arms tightened around her instinctively. 'Mmm…good morning.'

'Good morning.' She kissed a little lower, heading down towards his stomach, and Luca's eyes fluttered closed.

He should be tired. Exhausted, even. When they'd returned from the Piazzale Michelangelo the night before they'd fallen straight into bed and not emerged until they were starving. He'd whipped up a quick pasta dinner for them in the small kitchen of the apartment, but they'd barely finished eating it before they were on each other again, collapsing back into the bed with Daphne straddling his body.

He *should* be exhausted. But all he could think about was having her again.

He knew what this was. This was goodbye—for real this time. And he just wasn't ready for it. So he'd keep throwing himself into the phys-

194   A REUNION IN TUSCANY

ical distractions Daphne offered until it was over, and he went back to reality once more.

What else was there to do?

Her lips reached his bellybutton, the thin cotton sheet they'd finally fallen asleep under slipping away as she moved, and he felt her glorious breasts pressing against him and—

A sharp ringing noise interrupted the moment. And then it did it again.

'Sorry,' Daphne whispered against his stomach, and then she was gone, leaving him tense and wanting and confused, staring after her through the open doorway.

The ringing stopped. 'Dad? Is everything okay?'

His head dropped back to the pillow. Of course.

He heard a heavy sigh from outside the room. 'I'll be home tomorrow, Dad. I can't—'

Of course she would. That was the plan. The agreement. He'd just hoped she wouldn't be going right back into the same life she'd run away from. He'd hoped he'd given her the appetite for more.

Seemed he'd been wrong.

'Can't Caitlin—or Aunt Sharon—' Another sigh. 'Fine. I'll let you know when my flight gets in. But Dad—' She broke off, and there was another sigh. He heard her place her phone back down on the table in the hall. He must have hung up on her.

Luca waited a moment or two, but Daphne didn't return. After another few minutes, he smelled coffee brewing. The moment was well and truly ruined, it seemed.

He levered himself out of bed and into the bathroom, washing before pulling on a pair of pants and a T-shirt, and leaving the bedroom. His own phone was on the table beside Daphne's and he picked it up as he passed, swiping it open as he walked.

Daphne was sitting at the small bistro table by the window, two cups of coffee in front of her. He slid into the second chair, scrolling through his emails.

'That was your dad?' He tried to ask the question neutrally, although he wasn't sure how well he succeeded.

Daphne nodded. 'He was having some sort of crisis or another. I told him it'll have to wait until I get back. If it was really important there are other people—people who are in the same country right now—that he could call.'

That was a start, he supposed. He frowned as he saw an email from his manager with an all-caps subject heading.

WE NEED TO TALK ABOUT THIS!

He opened the email.

Call me as soon as you've read the below.

Across the table, he was faintly aware of Daphne taking a deep breath. 'Luca? I wanted to talk to you about something.'

'Sure.' He scanned down through the email, only half listening.

'I know I'm going home tomorrow…and I really do need to…'

Dear Mr Moretti,
We have reason to believe that you may be liable for—

Oh, hell, this wasn't going to be good.

'Sorry, Daph. I just need to make a call.' As much as he wanted to help her, he knew from her call that she was already slipping back into her old habits. She needed to break them herself—and she wouldn't appreciate him getting frustrated and telling her what to do.

Besides, he wasn't going to be able to concentrate on her decades-long problem until he'd tended to his immediate one.

His manager, Matilda, picked up on the first ring.

'Finally! Did you see this thing?'

Luca moved away from the table, drifting

back towards the small study he kept off the hallway as he spoke. 'Yeah, but explain it to me. These things always make more sense in your words.'

He heard the scrape of Daphne's chair on the floor behind him but, beyond that, had to focus on Matilda's words. As they started to sink in, he dropped into his desk chair and rubbed a hand over his forehead.

This was not going to be a good day.

It was a full twenty minutes before he was done with Matilda, and he returned to the lounge to find Daphne dressed and ready for the day, sipping another cup of coffee.

'Sorry about that.' His own coffee had gone cold and he looked longingly at hers. She picked it up and drank it, keeping eye contact the whole time. Luca smiled. Good for her. The old Daphne would have handed it over without a second thought.

Maybe she really was growing into the person she wanted to be. Except then there was that phone call from her dad...

'Is everything okay?' Daphne asked. 'The phone call, I mean.'

He sighed. 'No, not really. There's a problem with one of the property companies we were using in New York to find a site for a second restaurant. Apparently, they're now under investigation and we might be implicated, so I have to get back there right away to sort that out.'

'Right away?' Daphne echoed, and when he looked up her eyes were wide. 'Today?'

'I'm afraid so. You can stay here until your flight tomorrow, though—see anything else you want to. I'll arrange a car to the airport for you, you won't need to worry about anything.' He'd already rearranged her flight and paid the difference. 'I'm just sorry we have to cut this short, but I guess it means we don't have to worry about a long drawn-out goodbye, huh?'

As if this whole week hadn't been exactly that. From the moment he'd had her again he'd been counting down to losing her.

This really was for the best. He needed to get out before he fell any further. It would hurt to leave today, but it would only hurt more to leave tomorrow.

And he already knew what would hurt the most: hope. If they made promises to each other, and couldn't keep them. He couldn't risk that.

He had a business to get back to, people relying on him. He couldn't be distracted by... whatever this was between them now.

Because he knew it had gone way past nos-

SOPHIE PEMBROKE 199

talgia, far beyond goodbye. It wasn't a holiday fling—it never had been between the two of them. He was every bit as much hers as he'd been fifteen years ago, and her leaving then had almost broken him.

She was leaving again now, hopefully for a better life this time, one she actually wanted, like him. And he couldn't let her take his heart with her this time.

Which meant getting out of Florence as fast as possible.

'You're already flying back tomorrow, Luca. That's probably soon enough,' Matilda had said when he'd told her his intention of heading straight to the airport.

But he'd insisted he had to be there right away. He just hadn't been entirely open about the reasons.

And from the way Daphne was looking at him, with all that damnable hope in her eyes… he might have to lie to her too, if he wanted to get out of this with his heart intact.

He was leaving. Today.

She'd thought—hoped—that she had a full last day to find the right moment to talk to him about what happened next, about how maybe this didn't have to be goodbye. Not if they didn't want it to be. How maybe they could find a way…

It was the conversation they hadn't had before she'd left fifteen years ago. This time, she was trying to do better.

But now he was leaving—was already heading back to the bedroom to pack his stuff, talking about what she could do in Florence without him for the last day of her stay, and what time he'd book her car to the airport for, and she just couldn't.

She couldn't let him go without saying anything at all. But she also couldn't find the right words to do it now, in such a hurry.

Well, the wrong words would have to do, then.

She'd spent her whole life shying away from what she really wanted, not asking for her dreams because they were too much, or so far beyond what someone like her could expect. She'd let the other people in her life paint her into a box, tell her what she could and couldn't have, and she'd promised herself she wasn't going to do that any more.

Which meant she had to ask for what she really needed.

Use your words, Daphne.

She almost giggled at the thought; that was what Erin and Olly had said to their kids when they were small. She was at the emotional level of a *child* when it came to articulating her needs.

But everyone had to start somewhere.

'Luca—'

'I really am sorry I have to rush off like this,' he said, interrupting her before she could even start. 'But honestly, it probably is for the best. I'm sure you want some time alone to figure out what you're going to do next. I know I've been a distraction.' He flashed her a bright smile as he shoved clothes into his bag, but it didn't reach his eyes.

He was doing this on purpose. Why?

Luca had always been the one to encourage her to talk about her dreams, to follow her intuition and ask for what she wanted. So why wasn't he letting her talk now?

Because he's afraid of what you're going to ask for.

Was that because he wanted it too, and that scared him? No, it couldn't be. Luca was always the one who went after his dreams, no matter how daunting. Who took every chance and leapt at every opportunity.

If he was stopping her, it had to be for her sake. Because he couldn't give her what she wanted.

But she had to be certain.

'Luca. Before you go.' She grabbed his arm

202 A REUNION IN TUSCANY

and made him look at her. 'This… I know you have to go. But it doesn't have to be the end. Does it? I mean… I'm not asking for promises or anything. But maybe it shouldn't be fifteen years before we see each other again this time?'

Was she even making sense? She couldn't tell any more. She didn't know what she was asking for, what she was suggesting or offering. So how could he?

She'd thought she knew what she wanted, this morning, waiting for him to get off the phone. She'd thought she'd got it all sorted out.

But now, standing there with him looking pityingly down at her, she realised that all she'd done was figure out what she *didn't* want.

She didn't want to say goodbye. She didn't want this to end.

But she had no idea how that would work in their real lives, or what it would look like. They hadn't even talked about it as a possibility.

Not that it mattered, since it looked like Luca wasn't the least bit interested anyway.

He gently peeled her fingers away from his arm and stepped back, out of her reach. 'I don't think that's a good idea, Daph. I think…this week gave us the closure we need. The best thing we can do now is take it. Walk away and live our lives without looking back. I've got… responsibilities. And you've got a whole life to

SOPHIE PEMBROKE

go out and live—the last thing you want is anything or anyone else holding you back.'

He'd never tried to tell her what she wanted or needed before—he'd only ever helped her figure it out for herself. But now he was telling her that he knew best.

She hated it. But she couldn't tell him he was wrong. Especially when she still had so much to decide for herself.

It just felt too hard to walk away from this place without knowing if she'd ever see Luca Moretti again.

But if that was what he wanted… This wasn't giving in to someone else's whims. It was respecting their boundaries—and she hoped she'd always be able to do that.

She'd put herself out there. She'd tried. That was what mattered. If he didn't want this, didn't want her…she had to respect that.

'Right.' She forced a smile. 'At least we got that closure we were missing, hey?'

Relief flooded his expression. 'Exactly.'

She'd been right to leave without telling him fifteen years ago, she knew now. It meant she'd never had to live through this—the moment where she realised that, despite all his pretty words, and the way her body reacted to his, he didn't really want her dead weight pulling him down.

204 A REUNION IN TUSCANY

He'd said he'd loved her. That he'd been heartbroken when she'd left. But he'd gone on to live his life as if she'd never existed. Had it all just been to get her back into bed? To get another week of great sex with her before his real life came calling?

Anger started to rise and bubble in her chest as she pulled further away. He wanted this to mean nothing? Fine. This one last time she would give someone else exactly what they wanted, regardless of her own desires.

'And some half-decent sex isn't really worth travelling all this way for, is it?' she said, raising her eyebrows. 'It was fortuitous I was here anyway, but now…well, I've got better things to do with my life than revisit old memories. I'm ready to make new and better ones. Who knows, maybe I'll meet my next beau on the plane home. Someone new to learn from before I move on again.'

There was just the slightest wobble in his expression, but not enough to tell her what he was thinking.

'Well, thanks for the trip down memory lane, Luca.' She reached for her handbag, threw it over her shoulder and pressed a swift kiss to his cheek. 'Have a nice life, yeah?'

And then she turned and left, grabbing the

spare key on her way out, and leaving him speechless behind her.

Because at least this way she wouldn't have to watch him leave. And he wouldn't get to see her cry.

New York was worse than Luca remembered.

Maybe it was the late summer heat, or the smell, or the endless meetings to figure out what had gone wrong with the property deal.

Or maybe it was the way he spent every single damn minute wondering what Daphne was doing now. Who she was with. Whether she'd even thought about him at all.

He'd tried distracting himself. When he wasn't stuck in business meetings or working at the restaurant he'd made plans with friends, reminded himself what he enjoyed about his high-octane city life.

What he *used* to enjoy, anyway. Somehow, the shine had gone from club openings and VIP rooms, or even nights out at friends' restaurants.

The conversations seemed too superficial, yelled over too-loud music and interrupted by people wanting selfies with him. The women were too obvious, too…forward, he supposed, even though it made him sound a hundred years old. Everything about the nights out he indulged in after his return from Tuscany seemed to be about moving fast—eating new, exciting food rather than recipes that had been handed down through generations; meeting new, exciting people who he'd never get to really know, rather than spending time with people who knew and loved him, and whom he knew and loved in return; rushing through his days instead of enjoying them, and falling into bed at night with his mind overflowing and his heart quiet, instead of his heart feeling full and his mind quiet.

This wasn't the life he'd planned for himself, he realised suddenly, in the middle of a restaurant one night, surrounded by people he barely knew, eating Italian food that wasn't a patch on Aunt Rosa and Uncle Rocco's.

Except...except it *was*. His twenty-one-year-old self had absolutely seen this as the pinnacle of achievement. He was a success, feted by New York names, seen at the hottest places with all the beautiful people. He was on everyone's invitation lists, people stopped him in the street to be seen with him...

This was *exactly* what he'd wanted. Fame and success that outstripped his father's, and he'd done it all without him too.

So why didn't it feel like succeeding any more?

It hadn't, he realised, even before he'd gone

back to Tuscany that summer. Already, the experience had started to pale. He'd been talking with Matilda about new locations, next moves. What he could do that was bigger and better. Because that was how he'd handled this feeling every time before—he'd found the Next Big Thing that he could do to feel like he was succeeding. He'd moved on—to somewhere, something, someone new.

The problem was that it was starting to feel a lot like running away.

And for the first time in a very long time, he wanted to go *back* to something, not on to something new.

Maybe…maybe his dreams had changed. Maybe that was what it was.

He just needed to figure out what the new ones might be.

Luca swilled his wine around in his glass, his meal mostly untouched, ignoring the raucous conversations raging around him at the restaurant table. He was faintly aware of people taking photos surreptitiously on their phones from the tables around them, but that was only to be expected. He was dining with a Broadway star, a bestselling novelist, a columnist from *The New York Times*, an ex-ice-skating prodigy and at least two TV actors. Of course they were being watched.

208 A REUNION IN TUSCANY

He should probably be making more of an effort to look like he was enjoying himself.

When someone slid into the empty chair beside him—his original companion had long since swapped seats to join the more fun conversationalists at the other end of the table—Luca made an effort to look up and smile welcomingly.

His ex-girlfriend rolled her eyes. 'Don't *grimace*, Luca. That's hardly going to help our story, is it?'

'Our story?' He blinked at Serena uncomprehendingly as she tossed her long blonde hair over her shoulder. 'I thought our story was over, Serena.'

She scoffed. 'Hardly.' Adjusting the neckline of her fire engine red dress to reveal *more* cleavage rather than less, she positioned herself on the chair perfectly for the man at the table beside them holding his camera phone out. 'You're back in New York just in time for our big reconciliation scene.'

'We're not having one of those,' he said firmly. He might not be sure about much right now, but he was certain as hell about that.

The idea of falling back into a relationship with Serena that really only existed to serve the public attention, after everything he'd just shared with Daphne in Tuscany…it made him sick to his stomach.

Luca pushed away his hardly touched plate.

'And why, exactly, is that?' Serena's tone wasn't accusatory or cruel, he realised. She was rarely either of those things—she didn't care enough about him to be, he knew now. They were actors in a scene, except the scene was his life. When they were being observed she'd fawn over him, smile and laugh, touch his hand, his arm, his chest, his thigh…everywhere. But when the director called 'cut'—and no one was watching any more—she became a totally different person.

Actually, he liked *that* version of Serena far more. She was logical, acerbic and far more laid-back. But he'd always been exactly the same person whether they were being watched or not. He didn't know how to be anyone else.

I felt like someone else with Daphne, though. He pushed the thought away.

Serena didn't love him and he didn't love her, but they were a good fit all the same. He gave her the press attention she craved to keep building her career, and she gave him someone on his arm to distract all the other women who wanted his time, money, body or attention.

Or they had been. Now he'd been reminded

what a real relationship looked like he couldn't settle for what he'd had with Serena any longer.

Not that what he'd had with Daphne was a real relationship. It couldn't be. They both knew that.

Serena was watching him carefully, and the longer he didn't answer, the more amused she looked.

'Oh, my God, you've met somebody! Like, actually fallen in love! Haven't you?' She kept her voice low, but the excitement was clear. 'Luca! This is amazing!'

If Serena had ever had any real feelings for him, he was pretty sure she wouldn't be so happy for him. But since their relationship had only ever been for appearances—and even if it had involved her inviting the press to witness an orchestrated argument—she clearly wasn't bothered by his change of heart.

Literally.

'It's not amazing.' He reached for his wine glass. 'It's the worst possible thing that could happen.'

She stilled in her chair, no longer vibrating with excitement. 'Why would you say that?'

'Because love isn't what I need right now. That's not what this is about for us, is it?' He and Serena had always been on the same page about this, at least. 'You and me, we know that we can't have love *and* success. And right now I have to focus on my career, my business. I have so many people relying on me—in my restaurants, my publishers, my fans even. I can't take my eye off the ball and let them down.'

Look at Ben and Theo, for instance. Yes, they were making a great go of the cooking school at Villa della Luna, but they were still earning back the money to pay for the initial investment setting the place up. If they wanted to expand, set up a second site, build the business, he needed to keep his profile high, and keep the money rolling in. It was all business—even when it was family, and friends.

Serena's smile turned a little sad. 'Sometimes, I think you never knew me at all.'

'That's not—' He blinked a few times. Thought about everything he knew about Daphne after two weeks together, and everything he knew about Serena after a year. 'That might be true, actually.'

She reached out and took his hand. 'Luca, as much as I enjoyed dating you, we both knew it wasn't love, and that was fine. But you have to know, if real, true love had come knocking for me in the last year? I would have dropped you in a heartbeat to run after it. Publicity is one thing. But love? That's everything.'

'I never knew you were such a romantic,' he

said, mostly to hide the way his thoughts were tumbling in circles in his head at the revelation.

'Success and ambition and money... I'm not saying I don't want all that,' Serena said with a grin. 'But I don't see that love means I can't have it. I think that love would make it all even *more* worthwhile, because I'd have someone to share it with.'

'But what about *their* ambitions and dreams?' Luca asked. 'I can't ask...anyone to come follow my dreams instead of their own.' Especially as Daphne had already said no to that once, fifteen years ago.

Serena's expression was faintly pitying as she squeezed his hand. 'I think the idea is that you come up with new dreams and hopes. Together. For both of you.'

Well, of course it was. It seemed obvious now she said it.

Obvious, but not easy. Daphne had spent too long compromising on what she wanted. He *couldn't* ask her to do that again.

No, he'd done the right thing, leaving Florence when he had. For both of them. He had to hang onto that knowledge.

Sitting back, Serena let go of his hand and patted his fingers lightly. 'Look, I'm not saying love is simple or easy—if it was, we'd all have it already, right? But if you've found some-

SOPHIE PEMBROKE

one… Luca, you can't just walk away because you're too scared to risk being happy.'

'Why would I be scared of that?' Luca asked. He'd meant to sound mocking, but instead the words came out desperate.

Because he was, he realised. He was frightened of what Daphne made him feel. Terrified of losing it again if she left once more.

'Because if you're happy—truly, blissfully happy—you have everything to lose,' Serena replied.

Across the restaurant there was a bright flash—not just a camera phone this time. Luca glanced up in time to see a paparazzi photographer checking the viewing screen on his camera—and knew what he must have caught: him and Serena staring into each other's eyes and having a deep and meaningful conversation. Which meant that tomorrow's gossip pages were going to be all about whether he and Serena were back together again.

Perfect.

He just hoped that Daphne didn't see it.

CHAPTER TEN

DAPHNE HAD BEEN back in London for two weeks and already it felt as if she had never left.

Oh, she'd been trying—really, really trying—to implement all her best intentions about chasing her own dreams and living her own life for herself at last. And she'd made some changes! Just…she was more a one small step at a time person than a blow her whole life up in one fell swoop one, it seemed.

So she'd talked to Scott about taking on more responsibility at the shop, and her stepping back from being responsible for *everything*. She'd presented the resulting schedule to her father as more or less a fait accompli, and she'd do the same when she and Scott hired the new staff member they'd both decided they needed, too.

She'd enrolled her father in a food delivery service, and hired him a cleaner, both of which meant that, while she still made sure to spend time with him most days, that time was spent actually talking or watching something together, or even doing the crossword—rather than acting as his personal chef or housekeeper. With some of the new marketing strategies Scott had put in place over the last few months, the business was doing well enough that they could afford it.

She'd bought Tommy driving lessons for his birthday, which was really a gift for both of them. And she'd instigated a once a week catch-up with Caitlin at a cocktail-making class they were taking together—and inevitable drinks afterwards—and asked that Caitlin keep all the dramas she wanted to share for then so she could properly concentrate on them.

Small steps. But they were already making a difference.

She'd enrolled in a couple of night classes for the new term, starting in September—including an advanced one in Italian to take her beyond tourist level—but she'd also started making enquiries about more formal long-term study—the master's degree she'd always meant to go back and do, but never had.

And she'd started at least three different Pinterest boards for her future travel plans. So that was something, wasn't it?

The only problem was that none of it had,

A REUNION IN TUSCANY

in the slightest, lessened the ache in her heart from saying goodbye to Luca.

'How are you doing *really?*' Erin asked as she cleared away the bowls with the remains of their homemade pasta with a rich ragu. Not that there was much remaining—it had been delicious.

Across the table, Olly was watching Daphne with equally concerned eyes, which she assumed meant that Erin had told her husband everything. Their two kids, at least, had absconded from the table as soon as the garlic bread was finished, unbothered by their pseudo aunt's disastrous love life.

'I'm fine,' Daphne lied. 'Did I tell you about the cocktail class I'm doing with Caitlin?'

'You did.' Erin put down the pan and reached for the Parmesan cheese and grater. 'Are you seriously saying you haven't heard anything from Luca at all since you got back?'

Not counting photos of him with his ex-girlfriend—or possibly current again, the article wasn't sure—in the gossip pages, no. She hadn't. And she was fine with that. Mostly.

Daphne shrugged. 'Why would I? That wasn't the plan. I'm not even sure he'd know how to get in touch with me if he wanted to.'

'He could just ask Ben or Theo,' Erin pointed

out. 'All our details were on the booking form for the villa.'

'Well, that explains one thing, at least.' Daphne reached into her bag. 'I might not have heard from Luca, but I did receive this.'

She pulled the heavy cream envelope from her bag and passed it across the table to Erin.

'A wedding invitation?' Olly asked, watching as she opened it. 'Who's getting married? Oh…not Luca, surely? He wouldn't do that!'

Erin's husband was apparently very invested in Daphne's currently non-existent love life.

'Not Luca,' Daphne confirmed. 'Ben and Theo. They invited me to their wedding at the end of the month.'

'And are you going to go?' Erin asked, still admiring the invitation. Daphne understood the impulse—it really was a thing of beauty. The wedding would probably be spectacular.

'I don't know,' she admitted. 'I'm not sure if I should.'

Olly pulled a notepad from the kitchen counter behind him, tore off the shopping list on the front page, and drew a line down the middle of the next blank one. 'Okay, time for a pros and cons list.'

Daphne laughed. 'I think this is a little more complicated than our usual pros and cons lists. Not to mention that it was one of those damn

218 A REUNION IN TUSCANY

lists of yours that got me to Tuscany with Erin in the first place.'

'Exactly!' Olly beamed. 'And I maintain that was an excellent decision, romantic fallout notwithstanding.'

'You have to admit, you've been more…you again since you came home from Florence,' Erin said. 'Even if you never saw Luca again in your life, I still think those two weeks in Tuscany were worth it. They gave you your spark back.'

One spark in exchange for a broken heart. Daphne still wasn't sure it was a fair deal. 'Okay. Pros and cons.'

Erin went first. 'Pro: the wedding will be beautiful and you know it.'

'Con.' Daphne said, 'I won't know anyone there except the obvious and everything will be in Italian.'

Olly jumped in. 'Pro: it'll give you a chance to practise your Italian before your advanced course starts next month.'

'Con: I'll have to leave Scott to mind the shop *again,* and I've only just got back,' Daphne said.

'Pro: Scott loves the responsibility and it'll be good practise for you stepping back even more,' Erin replied.

'Con…' Daphne stumbled over trying to find

another con that wasn't 'Luca is the best man' because, of course, that was the main one, but somehow it still felt cowardly.

'Pro: It's very on-brand for your travelling more and getting out in the world resolution,' Olly said.

Daphne smiled with relief. 'Con: It doesn't count because I've been there before. Twice.'

'Pro: the food will be incredible,' Erin said, and they all just nodded at that as clearly there was no argument against it.

'The food is pretty great here too, though,' Daphne said desperately. 'I don't need to go to Tuscany for that.'

Erin gave her a look. 'Just say it, Daph.'

Daphne sighed. 'Con: Luca will be there.'

'Pro,' Erin shot back. 'Luca will be there.'

'It can't be both,' Daphne argued.

Olly tapped the pen against his cheek. 'I think it is. It's a con because you're afraid of seeing him again. But it's a pro because until you see him again, you're not going to move on, are you? I mean, you both seem to have spent fifteen years being emotionally held back by the end of your relationship the last time, so I can't imagine this one will be any different.' He leaned across the table to look her in the eye. 'You haven't said it, but you're in love with him, right? I mean, that's the impression

A REUNION IN TUSCANY

I get. And if you never face him again, never tell him…how are you going to move on?'

Daphne glared at Erin. 'Couldn't you have married one of those emotionally repressed men who'd have gone to the pub by now?'

'Sorry, no.' Erin pressed a kiss to her husband's cheek. 'And he's right. You know he is.'

'I know.' Daphne tipped back in her chair and closed her eyes for a long moment, thinking her way through the lists they'd made.

'You know, the first time he asked you to stay, you said no,' Erin pointed out. 'The second time you said yes. He's only said no to you once so far.'

She was right. Maybe she needed to ask him one last time.

At least then she'd know for sure.

And I did say I was going to go after the life I wanted from now on.

She'd give him one last chance, and then she'd move on. If he said no, that was it. But he'd have to say it to her face.

Daphne opened her eyes again and looked from Olly to Erin. 'So. I guess I'd better RSVP, then.'

He'd only been away from Italy for less than a month, but the sense of relief Luca felt driving up to Villa della Luna made it feel as if he'd been gone a lifetime.

Most of the guests wouldn't be arriving until the following day, which gave him a chance to catch up with Ben and Theo, go over his best man's speech a few times, and generally decompress before the big day.

It was strange, though, being back at the villa without Daphne again. Never mind that he'd spent far more time there without her than with her over the years, the place still felt as if something was missing without her there.

Or maybe he was the one missing something. Missing her.

Whatever it was, it was making him irritable.

After a mostly silent dinner with the grooms-to-be, Theo lost patience with him.

'Okay. Just to check. You do *realise* that you're bloody miserable, yes?' Theo asked.

Ben groaned and reached for the bottle of wine to top up their glasses. 'Love, we said we were going to let him deal with this in his own time.'

'But he *isn't*,' Theo said. 'It's been almost a month and the wedding is tomorrow and—'

Ben cut him off. 'And we'll all just have to see what tomorrow brings, won't we?'

Luca looked up. 'What do you mean by that?'

With an irritated look in Theo's direction,

222 A REUNION IN TUSCANY

Ben took over the conversation. 'We just mean that we're worried about you. As Theo pointed out so elegantly, you're not happy.'

'I said miserable,' Theo muttered. They ignored him.

'I'm not…unhappy,' Luca said. 'I just think I need to figure some things out.'

'Like how to win Daphne back?' Theo suggested.

Luca shook his head. 'That's not…on the cards. I just need a new challenge—professionally, I mean. New York has grown stale. I've achieved what I can there for the time being. So I need a new ambition. Something to get me fired up.'

Something to consume him, ideally. To take all his time and energy so he could stop thinking about how much he missed Daphne.

Ben and Theo exchanged a look. It wasn't a good look.

'What?' Luca asked.

'It's just…are you sure that's what you really need?' Ben asked.

'Why wouldn't it be?' Luca shrugged. 'It's always worked before.'

'Has it, though?' Ben pressed. 'I mean, fifteen years ago, fine, it made sense. You were heartbroken, you'd walked out on your father and your inheritance, you were finding your place in the world. Setting out to become a rich and famous chef was perfectly logical—well, for you, anyway.'

'But?' Luca asked, because he could feel it coming.

'But you already did that!' Theo burst out, as if he really couldn't keep it in any longer. 'You already conquered the culinary world, Luca! You proved your father wrong, you made your own fortune, you got over Daphne breaking your heart—the first time, anyway—you did it all!'

'What my beloved is trying to say,' Ben interrupted, 'is that you're always striving for the next thing, working harder for something more…but you never seem to just stop and enjoy what you have.'

'Except when you were here at the villa with Daphne,' Theo put in. 'And, if I had to guess, when you were in Florence with her too. Then, you just enjoyed the moment.'

'I…suppose,' Luca allowed. 'But it was a holiday. You're supposed to stop and smell the gelato or whatever on holiday, aren't you? That's not the same as the real world.'

'Since that's probably the only holiday you've taken in the last fifteen years, I suppose I'm impressed that you know that much,' Ben muttered.

'But why *can't* it be?' Theo asked. 'Why

224 A REUNION IN TUSCANY

can't you enjoy the real world just as much as a holiday?'

'I—' Luca realised his mouth was hanging open, and snapped it shut. He'd never thought about it that way before.

'Luca, Theo's right. Whatever point you were proving—to your father, or yourself, or Daphne, or whoever…you've made it.' Ben leaned across the table, placing one hand over Luca's. 'I know your father made you feel like you'd never be good enough. And maybe Daphne leaving back then made that worse. Maybe that's what made you keep trying harder and harder. But we're telling you—you're enough. Just as you are. Even if you hadn't achieved all you have, you would be enough. You're my best friend, and you're going to stand up beside me at the altar tomorrow as I marry the love of my life. And it's not because you're famous, or because you're an incredible chef, or even because you bought this villa to make sure I didn't lose it when my father went bankrupt, and gave me a purpose and a vocation when I had nothing.'

'Although that was pretty good,' Theo put in. 'Especially as it led to him meeting me.'

'The point I'm making is, none of that is why I asked you to stand up as my best man,' Ben said. 'I asked you because you're my best friend, and I love you, and I believe that who you are is enough. You don't have to do a damn thing to prove anything to anyone, okay? You can just…be for a while instead. I think you need it.'

Ben's words floated over him and as they sank in they seemed to bring a sense of relaxation, of relief, that Luca hadn't even realised he needed.

He was enough.

He didn't have to go back to New York and fight for the next big thing. He didn't have to fake a relationship to make the papers and keep his profile high. He didn't need to achieve and achieve and achieve to prove his father wrong.

He didn't have to put his ambitions, the things he thought he was supposed to do and want next, above what he really wanted.

Above love.

He could chase a new dream, just like Daphne.

How long had his friends been waiting to say this to him? How long had he kept his head down and ignored what was apparently obvious to everyone else?

He loved his career. He didn't want to give it up. But he didn't want it to be all he was any more either.

Luca let out a long breath. 'Not that I don't appreciate the reality check, but why are you telling me this tonight? The night before your wedding. Aren't there more important things you're supposed to be doing right now?'

'More important than my best friend?' Ben laughed. 'Never.'

'Besides,' Theo added, 'we invited Daphne to the wedding and she RSVP'd to say she's coming, so we figured we'd better get your head on straight before you saw her again.'

Luca's mouth fell open again.

'More wine?' Ben asked weakly.

Ben and Theo had arranged cars for all their guests from the airport to the villa, presumably to ensure that everyone arrived on time. The invitation had included a full itinerary for the day, and Daphne knew it was going to be a full one.

Since same sex marriages were still not legal in Italy, Ben and Theo would have been to the local town hall for their civil union ceremony that morning, with Luca and Theo's sister standing as witnesses. They'd chosen to keep that part of the day very private and small— just immediate family—as a contrast to the rest of the day's celebrations, it seemed.

Daphne was amused to find that she'd been given the same room at the villa as her last visit. She knew most guests were being ferried back off to other local hotels later that night, and was touched that Ben and Theo had thought to keep her close, since she'd be on her own.

That, or they were meddling. Now she thought about it, they were definitely meddling.

Still, with Luca down at the town hall with them, she had time to change into her outfit for the afternoon and do her hair and make-up after the flight. It was strange to be back there with so many other people arriving, but nobody yet that she knew. Strange, too, to be preparing for a wedding so much like her last night at Villa della Luna.

And they all knew too well how that one had ended.

Finally, she was ready and ventured out onto the terrace to watch for the grooms arriving. She'd promised herself that she wouldn't try to talk to Luca until after all his best man duties were performed—she didn't want to distract him, after all. This was Ben and Theo's day and she wasn't going to ruin it with her relationship drama.

Daphne smoothed down her terracotta dress, bought for the occasion because it reminded her of the Tuscan landscape in high summer, and leaned against the railings. The gathering was already in full swing, with a small crowd waiting around the rows of chairs with ribbons

228 A REUNION IN TUSCANY

and mini bouquets of lavender and olive leaves tied to the backs, laid out for the symbolic ceremony they had planned before the meal. With a deep breath, Daphne went to join them.

Soon, two cars with ribbons and flowers on them appeared on the road below, winding their way up to the villa, and everyone took their seats. Daphne found herself sitting with a gang of Theo's friends who were all in high spirits, and they muddled through a conversation in a mixture of languages.

Her heart started to tighten in her chest as she waited to hear the slam of car doors and the approach of the wedding party. She felt like a heroine in a romcom movie, waiting to stand up and say 'I object' at that moment in the wedding ceremony when the vicar called for any reasons for them not to be wed. Except Theo and Ben had already legally been joined in their civil union, and she wasn't here for them, anyway.

A chill suddenly fluttered down her back. What if Luca hadn't come alone? That photo of him with Serena that was doing the rounds… what if they *were* back together and he'd brought her as his date? That would kind of ruin all her plans, wouldn't it?

No. No, it wouldn't, she realised. Because she'd know.

Her only plan here was to make her peace with what she felt for Luca and move forward—with or without him. She wasn't here just for him, or to figure out what he wanted. She was here to decide what was next for her.

If he'd got back with his ex-girlfriend, that might actually make that easier. More heartbreaking, but easier.

It felt as if she'd spent fifteen years searching for closure from that summer in Tuscany, and when she'd thought she'd found it she'd discovered it wasn't enough. This time, though, she needed to do it for real.

And if she was lucky it might not be the end. It might be the start of something new instead.

But if it was the end? She'd survive. And she wouldn't hide again, living a small life for other people because she thought that was all she was worth.

Even if Luca never gave her another look, he'd given her that, and it was enough.

Suddenly, the string quartet at the front of the makeshift aisle struck up a tune, and the congregation turned as one in the ribbon-backed chairs to watch the wedding party arrive.

First came Ben's mother and stepfather—his biological father had categorically *not* been invited, she knew from conversations with Luca.

A REUNION IN TUSCANY

Then a couple who had to be Theo's parents, then presumably his sister and brother-in-law.

And then there was Luca, dressed in a perfectly tailored suit that accentuated his broad shoulders and his trim waist. He was smiling broadly, obviously happy for his friends, but his eyes scanned the crowd until—

His gaze hit hers and held. Daphne honestly thought her heart might have stopped.

Luca never missed a step. He made his way to the end of the aisle, but he kept his gaze fixed on her until he was past her seat and couldn't see her any more.

And Daphne sucked in a breath at last.

She was going to make it through this beautiful wedding. And then she was going to corner that man and sort out the rest of her life.

Because that hadn't been a look of surprise, or disappointment, or even the same sort of fear she'd seen in his eyes before they'd left Florence.

That look? That look was the same one she'd been giving him.

That look gave her hope.

CHAPTER ELEVEN

WEDDINGS WERE HELL.

Okay, no, Luca didn't mean that. Weddings were beautiful expressions of love and commitment and he was honoured to be part of his best friends' big day, but God, he just wanted it to be over already so he could find Daphne and straighten everything out at last and maybe, maybe earn himself a second—no, third—chance.

He wanted to tell her that he understood now. That dreams weren't something you could just throw yourself into and expect it to be easy. It hadn't been with his career, for all that he'd lucked out along the way. It had taken work—and a lot of faith and hope. Why had he imagined that love would be anything different?

He'd thought it couldn't work between them because they wanted different things, had different dreams to chase. He'd been scared to try

232 A REUNION IN TUSCANY

because what if he failed? What if he wasn't enough and she left again?

But if he'd thought that way when he was twenty-one he'd never have achieved any of his dreams. And a chance to be with Daphne, to see where things might go between them if they really committed to the dream…that was worth the risk, wasn't it? It was worth *trying* at least.

He just wanted to tell her that. To ask her if she'd try with him.

If he ever got the chance.

Best man duties overtook him for what seemed like for ever. He stole glances at Daphne every chance he got, watching her moving through the crowds of guests with a grace and confidence he'd always known was inside her, but hadn't always got to see. She seemed to have made friends with some of Theo's mates, which could be brilliant or terrible depending on how the rest of the evening went.

He made it through his speech without too much trouble, even though he was permanently distracted by the sight of Daphne several tables away, watching him. The speech was in Italian so he didn't know how much she understood, but it didn't seem to matter. She didn't look away, and so neither could he.

He'd accused Theo and Ben of meddling the night before, when they'd told him they'd invited her. He'd worried that she'd walk away again if he tried to talk to her. He deserved it, after how he'd left in Florence.

But now…he had to admit, maybe his friends had known what they were doing after all.

She'd watched him, walking down the aisle ahead of Ben and Theo. And she'd watched him through the speech. She'd been as focused on him as he was on her and that had to count for something, didn't it?

Maybe that third chance could be his. If he could just escape his best man duties and *talk* to her…

In the end, it was late in the evening, the sun long gone down, before he was able to catch her alone. The band Theo and Ben had hired for the evening were playing, and the same clearing had been laid with a temporary dance floor, just like the last wedding Luca and Daphne had attended together. That was probably a sign, Luca decided.

He should ask the lady to dance.

Except suddenly, having watched her all day, he couldn't find her.

He stood in the centre of the dance floor, spinning slowly in a circle, searching the crowds for her until—

A REUNION IN TUSCANY

A tap on his shoulder.

'May I have this dance?'

He turned and found her, looking hopefully up at him, and suddenly his voice was gone.

She was so beautiful in the starlight she took his breath away. His arms ached to be around her, and he knew that his heart wouldn't rest until she leaned her head against his chest and calmed it.

He knew he had so many things he wanted to say to her. So many things to discuss.

But all he could do right now was hold her. So he nodded and took her in his arms.

'This is familiar,' Daphne said, smiling up at him. And he knew what she was thinking— the last time they'd danced like this they'd promised themselves one more night together. Which had turned into one more week... But then her expression changed. 'Except... I don't want it to be. Luca... I didn't come here tonight looking for closure, and I want to be honest with you about that. If it's what I get, then fine. But... I promised myself I was done pretending to want what others want to keep them happy. I'm finished with making myself smaller, or more palatable, by going along with other people's dreams.'

'I'm glad,' he managed, his voice sounding rusty even to his own ears. There was more he should say, but Daphne was talking again before he could find the words.

'I tried to talk to you in Florence before you left, but I couldn't… I wasn't quite brave enough yet. So I put on a face, pretended I didn't want more than you'd already given me. That I was ready to walk away. But the last few weeks, without you, I've realised all the things I should have said. And being invited here tonight gives me the chance to say them, I hope.'

And now, even though he had his own things he wanted to say, his own apologies to make, he was far more interested in listening. Apart from anything else, he wouldn't dream of talking over her, or taking away her chance to speak. So he just nodded, and waited for her to continue.

The music played on and they swayed along to it, but Luca didn't think he could name that song if someone offered him a million dollars for it. All he could hear, see, think about was her. The scent of her lavender shampoo had filled his senses, the warmth of her skin against his threatened to overwhelm him completely.

'Fifteen years ago, I didn't want to leave you,' she said after a long moment. 'I had to, and it was the right thing to do, but I should have told you I was going, talked to you first. I honestly think the reason I didn't was that I couldn't believe I was that important to you. I know now that was wrong.'

Luca nodded, but still stayed quiet, as hard as it was.

'But you went out there and conquered the world, and I'm so damn proud of you for that,' Daphne went on. 'And when I saw you here again...it felt like a second chance to get it right. To find closure on that immature relationship that we'd never had. But what I found with you was so much more.'

She took a deep breath and Luca felt it against his body as they swayed together. Silently, he willed her on. Whatever she needed to say, whatever it meant for them, he wanted her to get it out. To ask for what she wanted at last.

He'd give her the world, if she let him. But she needed to ask for it first.

Not for him. But for herself. To believe that she deserved it.

That she deserved to be happy. Whatever that looked like, and however much work it took to get there.

'The week we spent together in Florence, and our time here at the villa before, they let me get to know you all over again—as a grown man this time, the man you'd become since we parted. And as much as I adored you at twenty-one…the man you are now, at thirty-six… That's the man I've fallen in love with.'

Luca stopped moving. If he froze, maybe he could preserve this moment for ever. Because right now he never wanted to leave it. 'Love?' he asked softly, unable to stop himself.

Daphne's cheeks turned pink, but she looked up and met his gaze anyway.

'Yes, love. I love you, Luca. I fell in love with you even though you told me outright not to. I love the way you make my world seem lighter. I love how you let your family tell me all the embarrassing stories they can about you. How you bought your friend a villa and a cooking school just to make him happy. I love the way you let me take the lead, that you give me space to figure out what I want. And I love that, when I'm done, you open up my eyes and my body to so many other possibilities. I love that you believe I deserve the world. That you think my dreams are worthy. But I also love that you don't think they're more important than yours.'

She took a deep breath and he felt it against his chest as he held her. 'I love you, Luca Moretti. And I think that maybe you fell back in love with me too. I know that love isn't everything. I know that you have lots of things in your life that matter more than I could. But I cannot move on with my life without you knowing. I love you. And if you decide to walk away from me, then I'll live, and I'll go on and have a great life, the same way you did when I left you. But if you say you love me too… maybe we could chase our dreams and build that great life together.'

He held her gaze, feeling the sincerity in her words, her eyes, and knowing that this, right here, was the moment when the rest of his life started.

And then he smiled.

All those motivational podcasts that talked about putting yourself out there, of speaking your truth and asking the universe for whatever it was you wanted…they had no idea how terrifying it was to actually ask for the one thing you needed most in the world—and then wait for the answer.

Daphne stared up at Luca's dear face and waited as he seemed to shake off whatever emotion it was that had made him stop stockstill and then…

And then he smiled. And Daphne's world came back into focus again.

'I love you too,' he said, shaking his head. 'Honestly, Daph, I'm not sure I ever stopped. But I was scared. I didn't think… I couldn't take the risk of you leaving again, of you putting everything else in your world ahead of what you wanted. I wanted you to have your own dreams, the future and life you wanted for yourself. I couldn't watch you give that up—even if it meant walking away from you to make sure you had the chance.'

'I won't,' she said firmly. 'Last time… I had to go home. But that didn't mean I had to give up everything. I know that now.' She could have talked to him, found a way to make it work, if she'd believed in their relationship—or in herself. She hadn't, then—but she did now.

She had a sudden flash of memory, listening to Luca and Ben talk in the kitchen the morning they'd left for Florence. 'What about you? I know you felt you couldn't have your career *and* love. Is that still the case?'

'No,' he said quickly. 'I… Ben and Theo talked some sense into me, along with others. I think… I think I threw myself into my career because it felt like something I could succeed at, far more than relationships or people did. Maybe because love is something you need to work at every single day, but you never, ever win. There's no end point. But maybe…maybe that's why it matters so much.'

'The loving is the winning,' Daphne said softly. Love wasn't a prize, wasn't something

240 A REUNION IN TUSCANY

to be claimed or won. It was something you *did,* day after day.

Something she wanted to do for the rest of her life.

'Yeah, the loving is the winning.' Luca smiled again. 'I like that.'

They weren't even pretending to dance any more, Daphne realised. Just standing under the Tuscan stars with a hundred other romantics, celebrating a day of love and togetherness.

The first of many, she hoped.

'So, what now?' Daphne asked. 'Last time we were here, we went to bed together, looking for closure. What are we looking for now?'

Luca's arms tightened around her waist. 'I think that's up to you to decide. I… I'm going to take a little time to enjoy my success for a while, before I come up with anything new to chase after. So if you wanted any company going after your dreams, I would be available.'

Daphne grinned. 'I think I could live with that.' She was already coming up with a list of places they could go, things they could see. Together.

'And longer term…well, that's up to you too. If you want to try this, see where it goes, no pressure, that's fine with me.'

That was the sensible path, Daphne knew. Really, they'd only known each other for one summer fifteen years ago, and two weeks now. There was no need to rush into anything. They should take their time.

Except, from one way of looking at it, they'd already been waiting fifteen years.

And Daphne didn't want to wait any more.

'Do you remember what you told me, the night we walked home from your family's restaurant?' she asked. 'When I asked you what I was to you, that summer? Who you thought I was?'

Luca frowned for a moment, then his expression cleared. 'I said I thought you were my for ever.'

Daphne leaned in and rested her cheek against his chest. 'Ask me who you are to me now.'

She felt his breath hitch before he asked, 'Who am I to you, Daphne?'

She looked up and met his gaze. 'I'm hoping you could be my for ever. If you'll have me. Want to come chase dreams with me and find out?'

Maybe it wouldn't work. Maybe they'd each find new dreams along the way—dreams they couldn't pursue together. But Daphne had a feeling this could be the start of something incredible. A dream she'd never even dared to dream before.

Either way, she wanted to find out.

'Always.' Luca dipped his head and brushed his lips against hers.

Somewhere, on the edge of the dance floor, she thought she heard Ben and Theo cheer. But she was too busy kissing Luca back to check.

Finally, they broke apart, breath coming hard, cheeks flushed and excitement racing through them.

'I guess our new dreams start today,' Daphne said, and Luca kissed her again.

Which was the best start to her new life that she could imagine.

EPILOGUE

One year later

LUCA LEANED AGAINST the edge of the terrace of Villa della Luna, coffee cup in hand, looking out over olive groves and the hills beyond. The morning was quiet but already warm and there was a buzz of insects in the air and a haze over the ground that told him the day was only going to get hotter. Inside, he could hear Ben and Theo rattling around in the kitchen, bickering good-naturedly over breakfast.

He took a sip of his coffee and waited.

A minute or so later, he was joined at the railing.

'What are we looking for?' Daphne ducked under his arm and stole his coffee cup. 'Our next adventure?'

Luca pressed a kiss to the top of her head. 'I thought you wanted some time here at the

244 A REUNION IN TUSCANY

villa before we headed out again. Something about planning…'

She flashed him a secretive smile. 'Well, yes. Have you told Ben and Theo yet?'

'Not yet,' he admitted. 'I'm waiting for the right moment.'

'Because it needs to be special or because you want to catch Ben so off-guard that he spits out his wine or drops something?' She knew him too well after a year together.

'Can't it be both?'

'I suppose.' She lifted her left hand up to the railing and let the morning sun sparkle off the diamond on her finger. 'I'm not going to keep hiding this for ever, though. It's too pretty not to show off.'

'That's fair.' It wasn't as if he'd given it to her only to keep it hidden. If it were up to him, Luca would shout it from the rooftops that she'd said yes. But they'd agreed there were certain people who deserved to know first.

He hadn't meant to propose so soon. They'd promised each other a year together to decide what happened next. He'd wanted to give them plenty of time to figure out what a life together would mean, how they'd both chase their individual dreams while still being in a relationship. Hell, when they'd started things again, he hadn't even known *what* he wanted to do next,

SOPHIE PEMBROKE

and Daphne was just starting out figuring out her own dream life.

But a year later…it had just felt right.

They'd spent their few months together zipping around all over the place. Daphne had been bouncing between London with her family and the shop, and visiting him in New York. She'd switched her evening classes to online, so she could take part in them from anywhere. She'd also set up her travel blog, writing first about Tuscany and New York. Her longform essays with their offbeat observations and evocative imagery—as well as some concrete recommendations about places to visit, including his family trattoria—had been popular from the get-go. And he wasn't above using his public image to get her more coverage either, mentioning her pieces on his own social media whenever they mentioned his or his family's restaurants.

Luca meanwhile had been hard at work setting up his business to run more or less by itself in his absence, or at least to the point that he had enough people who knew what they were doing that he could manage it via phone or email from wherever he was in the world.

It turned out then, when he wasn't always trying to do more, bigger and better and he trusted his staff to do the jobs he paid them for, Luca really wasn't quite so necessary to a lot of the proceedings. Which freed him up marvellously to go wherever Daphne wanted…

And so their real travels had begun.

He'd have happily paid for everything, but Daphne had saved enough over the years that she wouldn't let him. They'd picked their destinations by chance, spending time in one while Daphne learned enough to write an essay about it, then moving onto the next when the time felt right. They'd bounced around the globe for the better part of nine months, with occasional visits home to London, New York and Tuscany in between.

Luca had found the ring in an antiques market somewhere in Paris six months ago, and known already that it was the dream he wanted most in the world. So he'd bought it, hidden it in his bag and carried it around with him ever since, waiting for the perfect moment to present it to Daphne and ask her to spend all her future adventures with him.

But Paris hadn't felt right. Neither had the beach in Thailand at sunset. Or under the Aurora Borealis in Iceland. Or hiking in New Zealand, or the Grand Canyon, or Loch Ness, or any of the other incredible places they'd visited.

It was only now, when they'd returned to the

SOPHIE PEMBROKE 247

villa where it had all started, that he'd felt able to ask Daphne to marry him.

Now, on the terrace of Villa della Luna, Daphne studied her engagement ring curiously. Luca waited. He'd learned by now that these pauses, the moments when she seemed to be asking herself questions she couldn't answer in her head, really meant that she was preparing to ask *him* something.

'Did you mean what you said last night?' she asked finally.

'Which part?' He'd said a lot last night. His carefully composed proposal—honed over months on the road—had gone by the wayside and instead he'd just told her every little thing he loved about her until she'd put him out of his misery by kissing him then taking the ring from his fingers to place on her own hand.

'You said...you said that you wanted to start a new adventure with me.'

'That's right,' he said carefully.

'What...what sort of adventure were you thinking?' She sounded so cautious, so uncertain, it made his heart ache.

'Daph, in the last year, have I ever made that kind of decision alone?' he asked. She shook her head. 'Then, what sort of adventure do you *think* I was talking about?'

248 A REUNION IN TUSCANY

She blew out a breath and smiled up at him. 'One we decide on together?'

'Exactly.' He bent down to kiss her forehead and then her lips, just lightly. 'The most important thing I've learned about dreams this last year is that, as much as your dreams matter and my dreams matter, the ones that mean the most to me are the ones we come up with together.'

Maybe their marriage wouldn't look like other people's—like Ben and Theo's, happily holed up here at the villa. His life would always be partially in New York and, after a year out of the limelight, he was ready to start picking up some new projects again. And Daphne's home would always be in London with her family, as much as she loved to roam around the world.

So perhaps they wouldn't always be in the same place. Perhaps they'd travel apart as well as together. Maybe home would be a movable feast for them.

None of it mattered, he knew. Because they weren't living their lives for other people's dreams or expectations. Only their own.

'I love you,' he murmured against her hair. 'And that's the only thing that matters. What our life together looks like is up to us—and only us. And as long as we keep communicating, sharing our dreams...'

SOPHIE PEMBROKE

'We can be each other's for ever for good,' Daphne finished.

'Exactly.'

This time, he bent down to kiss her properly, and didn't stop until Ben called from the kitchen to tell them breakfast was ready.

'Come on,' Daphne said, grinning. 'I want to see if we can make Theo cry when we tell him we're having the wedding here.'

Because of course they were. Villa della Luna was where it had all started, and Luca hoped it would be a part of their lives together for a very long time.

'Come on then.' He gave her one last kiss, took her hand and led her back inside the villa.

It might have taken them fifteen years to get there, but for ever was definitely worth the wait.

* * * * *

If you enjoyed this story,
check out these other great reads
from Sophie Pembroke

Copenhagen Escape with the Billionaire
Christmas Bride's Stand-In Groom
Socialite's Nine-Month Secret
Cinderella in the Spotlight

All available now!

Harlequin Reader Service

Enjoyed your book?

Try the perfect subscription for Romance readers and get more great books like this delivered right to your door.

See why over 10+ million readers have tried Harlequin Reader Service.

Start with a Free Welcome Collection with free books and a gift—valued over $20.

Choose any series in print or ebook.
See website for details and order today:

TryReaderService.com/subscriptions